#Praise for @TeresaMedeiros and *GOODNIGHT TWEETHEART*

"Medeiros writes with effortless grace and addicitve wit about the importance of love and hope in every person's life."

—*Chicago Tribune*

"A very clever love story for the technological age!"
—*Fresh Fiction*

"Exactly the book to warm you up on a cold winter's night. . . . This novel will make you laugh out loud one minute and reach for the tissues the next."
—Kristin Hannah, *New York Times* bestselling author

"Measures out equal amounts of lightning-fast wit, wry intelligence, and haunting tenderness. Medeiros shows that in any era, by any means of communication, love will find a way."

—Lisa Kleypas, *New York Times* bestselling author

"Medeiros gives her well-matched Twitter couple some very funny exchanges."

—*Kirkus Reviews*

"A shrewd depiction of romance in an era of instant connection."

—*BookPage*

Also by Teresa Medeiros

The Pleasure of Your Kiss
The Devil Wears Plaid

Available from Pocket Books

TERESA
MEDEIROS

Goodnight Tweetheart

POCKET BOOKS

NEW YORK LONDON TORONTO SYDNEY NEW DELHI

Pocket Books
A Division of Simon & Schuster, Inc.
1230 Avenue of the Americas
New York, NY 10020

This book is a work of fiction. Names, characters, places, and incidents either are products of the author's imagination or are used fictitiously. Any resemblance to actual events or locales or persons, living or dead, is entirely coincidental.

Copyright © 2011 by Teresa Medeiros

First Pocket Books paperback edition September 2012

POCKET and colophon are registered trademarks of Simon & Schuster, Inc.

For information about special discounts for bulk purchases, please contact Simon & Schuster Special Sales at 1-866-506-1949 or business@simonandschuster.com.

The Simon & Schuster Speakers Bureau can bring authors to your live event. For more information or to book an event, contact the Simon & Schuster Speakers Bureau at 1-866-248-3049 or visit our website at www.simonspeakers.com.

Manufactured in the United States of America

10 9 8 7 6 5 4 3 2 1

ISBN 978-1-4516-5491-2
ISBN 978-1-4391-8817-0 (ebook)

To my beloved Twitter tweeps and Facebook friends and fans for making me smile every day and keeping me company along this amazing journey.

For my Michael, my very own Tweetheart. There is no greater blessing than wishing you goodnight every night of my life.

Acknowledgments

A hearty thank-you to Lauren McKenna, Louise Burke, and Andrea Cirillo for not having me committed when Mark and Abby started tweeting in my head.

Chapter One

*I*n her darker moments Abby Donovan had often fantasized that her career of choice might lead her to become intimately acquainted with the phrase "Would you like fries with that?" But she'd never guessed she'd end up embracing the traditional uniform of working women the world over—the bunny costume.

She'd started her morning safely tucked away in an upscale bookstore's version of a greenroom. It didn't look anything like the greenrooms at the *Today* show or even *Book World Weekly*. There were no comfy sofas or silver-plated trays of warm, gluten-free muffins and organic fruit. There were no fawning handlers asking if there was anything they could do to make her more comfortable while she waited for her cue to take the stage.

There was only a desk littered with mountains of yellowing publishing house catalogues and a creaky folding chair crammed between two towering stacks of boxes. Boxes of books that were probably going to be returned to the publisher for credit without ever being opened. The open door at the back of the room gave her an all too clear view of a bathroom that looked as if it hadn't been cleaned since the first season of *Survivor*.

Okay, so it wasn't really wasn't a greenroom at all, just an oversize storage closet.

Abby had sat hunched in the cold metal folding chair while she waited to be summoned, nervously eyeing the boxes of books and wondering how long it would take someone to find her if they toppled over on top of her. Despite the soothing strains of what sounded like *The Worst of Yanni* being piped through the overhead speakers, her nerves were jittering like she'd had a triple shot of espresso in her Skinny Caramel Macchiato instead of her usual double. She'd never been particularly prone to stage fright, but lately just the prospect of leaving her apartment for a trip to the corner bodega made her break out in icy beads of flop sweat. She stole a look at her watch, then sighed.

Maybe they figured if they left her there long enough, she'd start scrubbing the rust stains from the cracked vinyl around the toilet bowl.

Desperate for something to occupy both her

hands and her mind, she reluctantly lowered her gaze to the book lying in her lap.

The perky little gold seal on the front of the dust jacket announced to the world that both the book and its author were Something Special. That they had been chosen. Annointed. Smiled down upon by the benevolent goddess of Mount Harpo herself—Oprah Winfrey.

Being chosen for Oprah's book club was a little like being struck by lightning at the precise moment you won the lottery. It left you dazed by your own (presumably undeserved) good fortune and basking in a spotlight that faded all too quickly, leaving you blinded by its glare. Like most lottery winners, you were likely to end up going bankrupt within six months. And like most people who are struck by lightning, you had a ninety percent chance of survival, but you were never going to be exactly the same.

Four years later, Abby was still waiting to see if she would make it.

Hoping to avoid the humiliation of being caught reading a book she had authored, she flipped the book over. A younger, glossier version of herself smiled up at her from the back of the dust jacket. It wasn't hard for her to eye the photo with the critical eye of a stranger. The publicist provided by her publisher had chosen her wardrobe, her makeup, even her hairstyle for the photo session. It had taken the stylist over an hour to tame her naturally curly bob into a shining cap of golden brown hair.

She could still remember the Italian photographer urging her to try to look sensitive, successful, and vaguely sexy all at the same time. In hindsight, Abby thought she looked unbearably smug and vaguely constipated.

"Mrs. Donaldson?"

Abby sprang guiltily to her feet, fumbling for the book before it could slide onto the floor. Being caught mooning over your own picture was only slightly less humiliating than being caught reading your own book.

"Ms. Donovan," she corrected, remembering enough of her social graces to fix a cheerful smile on her lips. "Abigail Donovan. But you can call me Abby."

Her long-awaited deliverer was a tall, thin creature in a faded Coldplay T-shirt. The girl's asymmetrical haircut had been dyed Elvis black and accented with a bright shock of purple bangs.

Despite the pierced eyebrow, the tattoo of a fearsome serpent wrapped around her wrist, and the name tag branding her as "Natalie" (which assured bookstore customers she was there to help them), the girl didn't look old enough to be reading Harry Potter, much less selling it.

She popped her chewing gum, eyeing Abby with the sullen air of cynicism that could only be achieved by those with nothing to be cynical about. "The manager sent me to tell you it's time for your reading, Miss Donnelly."

This time Abby didn't waste her breath correcting her. Instead, she dutifully followed the girl's nonexistent rear end in its size zero Gap jeans from the room, giving the hem of her own sweater a furtive tug to make sure it was still hiding the waistband of her Spanx.

She had chosen her attire with great care. In the past few months she'd grown far too comfortable in the blocked writer's uniform of fuzzy socks and coffee-stained sweats. The tasteful beige of her cashmere mock-turtleneck sweater perfectly complemented the warm chocolate hue of her wool pencil skirt. She had even invested in a shiny new pair of Stuart Weitzmans, hoping the flirty pair of nude pumps would scream *successful beyond your wildest dreams* instead of *desperate to recapture former glory*.

As they traveled down a short hallway lined with cluttered cork bulletin boards, Abby heard a sound she hadn't heard for a very long time—the excited murmur of voices and the rustling of a crowd growing restless with anticipation. She relaxed her death grip on her book, her confidence growing with each step. Apparently, she had wasted her time and her energy worrying over nothing. Her readers had always flocked to her signings and readings in the past. She should have known they wouldn't forget her so quickly. A gracious smile curved her lips as she prepared to greet them.

She followed her escort right into the unforgiving glare of the overhead fluorescents. The rustling died and a collective sigh of disappointment washed over her. Her eyes adjusted just in time to watch the hope fade from the dozens of tiny little faces turned in her direction.

"She's not Biff!" a high-pitched voice wailed.

"You're right, Brandon," a deeper voice crooned. "She's nobody. But if you'll be a good boy for a little while longer, Biff will come hopping along *very* soon."

That's when Abby realized they hadn't emerged among the racks of overpriced stationery and tasteful displays of Godiva chocolate she had passed on the way in, but in the children's section of the bookstore. And that the large crowd—composed exclusively of fidgeting preschoolers and a handful of long-suffering parents—wasn't waiting for her.

An enormous banner hung over their rapt little heads. It featured a watercolor illustration of a rather fey-looking rabbit in a flowered apron serving tea to a gathering of forest creatures that included a shy fawn and a simpering hedgehog. According to the elaborate script etched across the top of the banner, their gracious host was none other than *Biff the Bunny*.

"My publicist didn't mention there was another event scheduled for today," Abby murmured to Natalie as she was forced to step over a sulking toddler huddled on a beanbag chair shaped like a toadstool, then duck beneath the bottom of the banner to avoid being slapped in the face.

Although she hated to admit it, even to herself, she'd been so excited to hear from her publicist after having the woman duck her phone calls for nearly a year that she probably wouldn't have noticed if she'd been informed the store had booked a spectral Margaret Mitchell to sign *Gone with the Wind*.

"Didn't you see the full-page ad we ran in the *Times*?" the clerk asked her.

"Um . . . no. But my publicist did fax over the in-house newsletter featuring my upcoming appearance." Abby's picture had been so small she'd had to squint to recognize herself.

"Well, Claire Carroll, the author of *Biff the Bunny,* is coming to do a reading today. She dresses up as Biff and reads her stories to the kids. The kids eat it up and most of the parents use it as an excuse to dump the little monsters on us so they can go blow their credit limit at Restoration Hardware. They were lined up outside the doors before dawn this morning."

Abby stole a glance over her shoulder at Biff's eager audience, wondering if she'd actually sunk so low as to be jealous of a fictional rabbit. She nearly walked into Natalie's back as the girl stopped in front of a swinging metal door situated just behind the Alternative Sex section.

"Here you go. We've got you all set up in the conference room."

Right before the clerk swept open the door, Abby caught a glimpse of a piece of college-ruled notebook paper taped to it. The words MEET THE AUTHOR had been scrawled on the paper, along with her name and the title of her book. There was no mention of the book being an Oprah pick. No hint that she had come *this close* to winning the Pulitzer.

The conference room was long and narrow. A battle-scarred podium with a drooping microphone attached to it sat on the right side of the room. Someone had optimistically arranged two dozen metal folding chairs in a semicircle around the podium. Only one of those chairs was occupied.

An elderly man wearing a pair of hearing aids was slumped in the chair, idly flipping through a copy of Abby's book. Judging by his exaggerated yawn, he was not impressed with what he found. Or it was time for his afternoon nap.

Ignoring the abrupt plunge of her heart into the toes of her overpriced pumps, Abby squared her shoulders. If she'd learned anything from being the only daughter of an army drill sergeant and a bipolar mother, it was that the show must go on. An audience of one was still an audience. If this man cared enough to attend her reading, then he deserved a performance worthy of Carnegie Hall.

Natalie began to back toward the door. "I'll be right outside if you need me. I have to go help my boss herd the rug rats. A couple of kids were nearly trampled at Biff the Bunny's last appearance."

Abby was still marveling over the fact that a rabbit named Biff could generate carnage previously only equated with a Who concert when the old man jerked to attention, his head swiveling around like Linda Blair's in *The Exorcist*. "Biff the Bunny? *Biff the Bunny is going to be here?*"

He sprang to his feet and rushed past them, leaving the metal door swinging in his wake. Abby and Natalie stared stupidly after him for a moment before shifting their wide-eyed gazes back to each other. Natalie tucked a pinkie between her lips, her world-weary facade cracking just long enough to reveal a trace of compassion . . . or was it pity?

Noting that the rest of the girl's black-painted fingernails had already been gnawed down to the quick, Abby managed a you-win-some/you-lose-some shrug for her benefit. "It's all right. Really. Who doesn't enjoy a nice subway ride to Queens on a sunny Saturday afternoon? Besides, writers can never spend enough time in bookstores, can they? I'll just hang around for a little while. Browse the New Book section. Or maybe the Alternative Sex section. These days one never knows when one might need to find an alternative to sex." She blinked rapidly, desperately wishing she hadn't left her faux Hermès bag—and her knockoff Prada sunglasses—locked in a desk drawer in the storage closet.

Natalie hesitated, plainly torn between her sympathy for Abby's plight and her desperate desire for escape. Before she could bolt, the metal door came swinging open again. A heavyset woman with short-cropped sandy blond hair came sweeping in. She wore a rumpled blue polo shirt, neatly pressed khakis and a name tag that identified her as Inga, the store's manager. Her broad Teutonic face was flushed and she had a shapeless lump of fur that looked like the deflated carcass of a German shepherd draped over one arm.

"Natalie!" the woman exclaimed, her relief nearly palpable. "There you are! Thank God! What size do you wear?"

"Zero," Abby said at the exact moment Natalie said, "Two."

"Oh, crap." The woman's face fell as she gave the carcass draped over her arm a despairing look. "This thing would swallow you whole."

Abby eyed the mangy wad of fur dubiously. "It looks as if it's already swallowed more than one victim."

The store manager blinked at her owlishly from behind the rims of her oversize glasses. "Who are you?"

"This is Mrs. Davenport," Natalie informed the woman before Abby could reply. "You know—the lady who was supposed to do the other reading today."

Abby extended her hand. "Abigail Donovan. I'm so glad to have the opportunity to thank you for your hospitality."

The woman swept her dazed gaze over the empty half circle of chairs. "You must be finished."

"You might say that," Abby said dryly, letting her hand fall back to her side.

The manager blinked several times in quick succession, as if to snap herself out of a trance. "I hope you'll forgive me for pawning you off on Natalie here, Miss Donovan. I'm just so flustered today. It's not often the store gets a visit from an author as successful as Claire Carroll, especially way out here in Queens. Most of the major publishers send their big names to the stores in Manhattan." As Abby's already pained smile vanished altogether, Inga froze with her fingers still curved into the air quotes she had used to emphasize *big names*.

Before she could stammer out an apology that would only embarrass them both, a collective groan drifted through the door. It was the tragic sound of dozens of tiny hearts breaking all at once.

The manager slumped against the wall, adding her own groan to theirs. "Oh God. What am I going to do? It's Claire Carroll. I've been on the phone with her publicist all morning. Her flight from Bermuda has been delayed. She's not going to make the reading." She raked a hand through her hair, leaving it standing on end. "I just had Stefan tell them Biff the Bunny was going to be late. I was afraid to tell them she—I mean *he*—wasn't coming at all. What if they riot?"

Mentally assaulted by an image of raging preschoolers swinging from that obscenely large banner and hurling their beanbag toadstools at a SWAT team in full riot gear, Abby had to bite back her first genuine smile of the day.

"I'm so sorry," she said, turning toward the door. "I should probably just go and get out of your way so you and Natalie can deal with this problem without any distractions."

"Wait!"

Abby turned back to discover a shrewd glint had overtaken the panic in the manager's eyes. "What size are you?" the woman demanded.

That's when Abby realized the limp carcass draped over her arm wasn't roadkill scraped off the Queensboro Bridge after all, but a Biff the Bunny costume, probably shipped directly from Claire Carroll's publisher so it would be there in time for her appearance.

"Oh no," Abby said, shaking her head and backing toward the door. "You can't ask me to impersonate an author."

"You wouldn't be impersonating an author because you *are* an author," the woman pointed out, her voice softening on a wheedling note. "You'd be impersonating a bunny. All you'd have to do is read *Biff the Bunny's Adventures in Carrotland* and hand out some candy. How hard would that be?"

"But I didn't come here to read *Biff the Bunny's Adventures in Carrotland*," Abby protested, her own desperation growing. "I came here to read *my* novel." She flipped the book in her hand around, hopefully displaying her literary equivalent of a glamour shot. "You know—the one *I* wrote."

Natalie shook her head disapprovingly and popped her gum. "I don't think the rug rats would like that. Last week one of the parents threatened to sue Corporate because we let the story hour volunteer read *Where the Wild Things Are*. Claimed the Things were too wild."

The manager seized Abby's arm, having saved her most persuasive argument for last. "If I could squeeze my ass into this thing, don't you think I would?"

Abby closed her eyes to escape the woman's pleading look, but all she could see was a circle of hopeful little faces shining up at her. The little boy in the children's section had been right. She wasn't Biff the Bunny. She didn't even seem to be Abigail Donovan the Bestselling Novelist anymore. She was nobody. But it was still within her power to keep the dreams of those children alive. To preserve their innocence for just a little while longer so they could believe a fey bunny who wanted nothing more out of life than to tend his carrot garden and have tea with his friends could actually survive in this ruthless world.

Opening her eyes, she tossed her own book into one of the folding chairs, where it promptly slid facedown onto the floor, hiding Oprah's seal of approval.

"Where can I change?" she asked grimly, already knowing the answer before Natalie Who Was There to Help Her and the grateful manager began to wrest her cashmere sweater over her head.

Chapter Two

Abby stabbed the button for the ninth floor, then slumped against the elevator wall. The doors slid closed, making her wince as her reflection came into view in their polished brass surface. She looked exactly like a woman who had spent her morning trapped in the suffocating confines of a bunny costume being heckled, stomped on, and repeatedly groped by savage little hands. She'd sweated off every last drop of her artfully applied makeup and contracted a terminal case of bedhead.

She'd received only the most cursory of glances while trudging up Fifth Avenue from the Fifty-ninth Street subway station in the bright April sunshine. She could have probably been hopping along still wearing the bunny suit and nobody would have noticed. This was Manhattan, after all. One sweaty, shell-shocked writer could hardly compete with a Kid Rock lookalike wearing nothing but a pair of tighty whities and a smile while he played guitar in the middle of Times Square.

The low point of her day had come when an overzealous mother had plopped her chubby little girl down on Abby's lap. Gawking at Biff's exaggerated whiskers and floppy brown ears in abject terror, the toddler had screwed up her angelic face and let out a piercing wail. As a suspicious dampness began to seep through the fur over Abby's knee, it was all she could do not to burst into tears herself.

The elevator doors slid open and she went limping down the hall to her apartment. To add injury to insult, her new Stuart Weitzmans had rubbed a painful blister on the back of one heel.

She fished her Robot Chicken keychain out of her purse and let herself into her apartment. She triple deadbolted the door, then collapsed with her back against it as if to ward off a horde of marauding preschoolers.

Three years ago, when still riding high on the wave of her newfound fame, paying $6,500 a month to rent a 695-square-foot apartment in the glorious old building once known as the Plaza Hotel had seemed like a perfectly sane idea. After all, what kid who had ever read *Eloise* hadn't dreamed of romping through the venerable halls of the Plaza while everyone else was asleep? And what writer hadn't imagined penning their latest masterpiece while overlooking the sweeping green expanse of the most famous park in the world?

What the apartment lacked in size, it made up for in chic. The kitchen, living room, and sleeping area might share the same long room, but it was painted a tasteful taupe and beautifully lit with a sparkling Baccarat chandelier. To the French countess who had sublet it to her, it was just one pied-à-terre among many scattered throughout the most exotic cities in the world. To Abby, it was home.

Even though she knew her days there were as numbered as the zeroes in her shrinking checking account, returning to her cozy little nest still gave her a rush of pleasure.

Her lips softened in a smile as her two fluffy gray cats came trotting up to greet her. As long as Buffy the Mouse Slayer and Willow Tum-Tum were around, there would always be someone happy to see her.

The cats took one horrified look at her, then wheeled around and went careening away to seek refuge in the bathroom. Abby sighed, the last of the fight going out of her. She probably smelled even worse than she looked.

She was desperate for a scalding shower, but at the moment even the simple act of dragging herself into the bathroom and turning on the water seemed like a monumental task.

She tossed her bag onto the sleek leather Bottega Veneta sofa chosen for her by an overpriced decorator, tugged off her shoes, and padded over to the desk in front of the window. Sinking into her task chair, she flipped open the screen of her MacBook.

Her e-mail inbox was populated by the usual suspects. A dozen fellow writers bemoaning the wretched state of the industry. A couple of investment bankers bemoaning the wretched state of their industry. A friend who worked for the post office bemoaning the wretched state of his industry. A generous Nigerian requesting her checking account number so he could deposit millions of tax-free dollars into her account. Someone promising her a lower mortgage rate, cheaper prices on Canadian drugs, *and* a longer-lasting erection—the holy trinity of modern happiness.

She was about to close her inbox when a joyful ding heralded the arrival of another e-mail.

Abby flinched. It was from her publicist.

She cautiously clicked it open, wondering if one of the parents at the bookstore had somehow managed to recognize her in the bunny costume and posted the most humiliating moment of her life on YouTube.

Hillary's tone was as doggedly cheerful as ever. As she scanned the message, Abby could not help reading between the lines:

Hi Abby,

I hope your appearance today was a smashing success! At this point, I don't feel like we can afford to overlook any opportunity to get you in front of the public. (Even if that public consists solely of incontinent toddlers.) I hope you don't mind, but I also took the liberty of signing you up for a Twitter account today. (Because you obviously can't be trusted to do it yourself any more than you can be trusted to finish Chapter Five of your new book.) A lot of our writers (you know—the ones who are still actually writing) are finding Twitter a great way to maintain a rapport with their readers without investing much time or creative energy. (They use their hefty royalty checks to hire assistants who impersonate them online while they finish their books on time.) I've attached your log-in info below. I think this will be a great way to make sure your devoted readers don't forget you! (Or at least the three devoted readers who haven't already forgotten you.)

The smiley face emoticon at the bottom of Hillary's e-mail appeared to be smirking at her. It obviously knew what Hillary was refusing to admit, which was that Abby could write countless blogs, send out insufferably cheerful monthly e-newsletters that made her life sound more fascinating than John Mayer's, and post a hundred Facebook updates an hour, but it still wouldn't stop *her* readers from flocking to the next hot new literary phenomenon. Especially if she proved to be nothing more than the publishing industry's equivalent of a one-hit wonder—a possibility that grew more likely with each passing day.

She glanced at the log-in information Hillary had sent. Several of her writer friends were already all abuzz about Tweeter or Flitter or Titter or whatever the heck it was. From what she could gather, it involved communicating only in sound bytes that consisted of 140 characters or less.

Prompted more by reluctance to haul her weary body into the bathroom than out of genuine curiosity, Abby clicked on the link Hillary had sent, then used the log-in information to access her account.

According to the page that popped up, she was now "Abby_Donovan" and she already had seventeen Followers. Having "followers" made her feel like some sort of kooky religious cult leader. Instead of using her pub photo as her profile pic, Hillary had left it a neutral brown square. Which pretty much summed up the way she was feeling at the moment.

An empty box invited her to answer one simple question—"What's happening?"

Her fingers hovered over the keys, torn between typing "None of your business" and "I'm throwing myself a pity party. Bunny costume optional."

Hoping her readers would possess both a sense of humor and a sense of irony, she finally settled on, *"I'm sipping Cristal on the beach at St. Tropez with Brad Pitt."*

Nothing. Apparently users of Twitter had better things to do with their time than applaud her shallow witticisms.

She drummed her fingers on the MacBook's touchpad for a minute, then typed, *"Halloooo...? Is anybody out there?"*

She refreshed her screen two times in quick succession. Still nothing. She decided to try one more time before retreating to the steamy oblivion of the shower. A message popped up on the screen, rewarding her persistence: *"R U a virgin?"*

Taken aback, Abby studied the cheery little profile pic of a plump bluebird that appeared to belong to one MarkBaynard for a long moment before cautiously typing, *"That depends. Are you audition-*

ing for TO CATCH A PREDATOR?" and hitting the Update button.

MarkBaynard's response was almost immediate: *"Glad to see you have such highbrow taste in entertainment."*

A reluctant grin curved her lips as she typed, *"What can I say? ROCK OF LOVE: TOUR BUS reruns can't be on every night."*

"Yeah & who hasn't dreamed of marching up to some pedophile & saying 'My name is Chris Hansen from DATELINE NBC & your sorry ass is toast'?"

"Ha!" Abby typed, hitting the exclamation mark with a triumphant flourish. *"So you HAVE watched TO CATCH A PREDATOR!"*

"Only when PBS is having a pledge drive. But I digress—R U a Twitter virgin?"

"This is my first time," Abby confessed. *"But you're not being very gentle with me."*

She was growing increasingly comfortable with the rhythm of their exchange on the screen. It was like being in a tennis match with their words as the ball. Before she could draw back her racket, he lobbed another volley across the Internet:

MarkBaynard: What can I say? I like it rough. So how did you end up here? Attention span too short for Facebook?

Abby_Donovan: I didn't like the answers to those silly Facebook quizzes. They kept telling me I was the love child of Marge Simpson & Marilyn Manson.

MarkBaynard: Maybe you're just secretly one of those people who would rather have Followers than Friends.

Abby_Donovan: Yes, it's part of my diabolical plot to achieve world domination.

MarkBaynard: If you start hanging out over here, won't your Facebook Friends miss you?

Abby_Donovan: Those people weren't my friends. If they had been, they wouldn't have sent me all those annoying quizzes.

MarkBaynard: A true friend never asks you to feed their imaginary fish. Or fertilize their imaginary crops.

Abby_Donovan: Although with a little coaxing, I might be persuaded to take home your imaginary kitten. So how is Twitter different from Facebook?

MarkBaynard: Twitter is the perpetual cocktail party where everyone is talking at once but nobody is saying anything.

Abby_Donovan: Then why are YOU here?

MarkBaynard: Because no one will invite me to their cocktail parties.

Abby_Donovan: I can't imagine that. Not with your warmth, wit, and charm.

MarkBaynard: Well, if you must know, I was considering a career as a DEmotivational speaker.

Abby_Donovan: And just how would that work?

MarkBaynard: You get a fabulous, innovative new idea, then pay me to come to your house and explain why it'll never work.

Abby_Donovan: What time can you be here?

Abby leaned back in her chair, bemused by how quickly she had been drawn into a conversation with a total stranger. Before he could reply, she started typing again.

Abby_Donovan: How do I know you're not a serial killer or some lonely 14-year-old living in your mom's basement?

MarkBaynard: For all you know, I'm a lonely 14-year-old serial killer living in my mom's basement.

Abby_Donovan: With your girlfriend's head in the refrigerator?

MarkBaynard: That would be my EX-girlfriend, thank you very much. I tried to tell her I didn't care for cream in my coffee. Or wire hangers.

Abby_Donovan: Is that your mom I hear knocking on the basement door?

MarkBaynard: No, it's the police. Did you just call 911?

Abby_Donovan: C'mon...who are you really? Are you hiding a secret identity? Are you Batman? Ashton Kutcher?

MarkBaynard: Would you believe I'm just a lowly college professor on sabbatical?

Abby_Donovan: Let me guess. You've taken a year off from teaching English lit at Cornell to travel the world and write the Great American Novel (snort).

Abby waited. She refreshed the page half a dozen times, but still nothing. She felt oddly relieved when the bluebird reappeared.

MarkBaynard: If you must know, I've taken a year off from teaching English lit at Ole Miss to travel the world and write the Mediocre American Novel.

Abby_Donovan: Oops. My bad. I'm Abigail Donovan, the author. But you can feel free to pretend you've never heard of me if you like.

MarkBaynard: Um...that shouldn't be too hard...since I've...um...never heard of you.

Abby_Donovan: Oh. Reading limited to SPORTS ILLUSTRATED SWIMSUIT EDITION?

MarkBaynard: And the special double Christmas issue of JUGS.

Abby_Donovan: I'm not quite sure how all this works yet. I just assumed you were one of my Followers.

MarkBaynard: I am now. Your name popped up when I just happened to be trolling Twitter looking for new vic—um...friends.

Abby_Donovan: So...now that we've successfully humiliated each other, maybe we should start over.

MarkBaynard: Why not? So what are you wearing?

Abby_Donovan: I was wearing a bunny suit earlier today.

MarkBaynard: Playboy?

Abby_Donovan: Biff.

MarkBaynard: Ah, does this mean you'll be expecting Felicity the Fawn and Biff's main squeeze Henrietta Hedgehog for tea this afternoon?

Abby_Donovan: Given Biff's fondness for paisley and PROJECT RUNWAY, I just assumed that would be Henry the Hedgehog.

MarkBaynard: Henry/Henrietta likes to take advantage of Biff's "Don't ask, don't tell" policy.

Abby_Donovan: So you've actually heard of that wascally wabbit and his furry little posse?

MarkBaynard: Hasn't everyone? After all, he inhabits the exalted toddler stratosphere formerly occupied only by Barney the Dinosaur and Tinky Winky.

Abby_Donovan: At least Tinky Winky had an inkling of fashion sense. Biff wears an apron and no pants.

MarkBaynard: Who are you kidding? Tinky Winky's purse looked like something Queen Elizabeth would carry.

Abby_Donovan: Somebody peed on me today. I bet nobody ever peed on Queen Elizabeth. Or Tinky Winky.

MarkBaynard: How do you think he got the name Tinky Winky?

Abby_Donovan: So what are YOU wearing?

MarkBaynard: The trench coat and fedora Bogie had on when he said good-bye to Ingrid Bergman on the tarmac in the last scene of CASABLANCA.

Abby_Donovan: Sigh…we'll always have Twitter.

MarkBaynard: I'm afraid not. I have to go now.

Abby_Donovan: Oh. Well, tell your mom I said hi. Or your parole officer.

MarkBaynard: If you'll log on Monday around 3 p.m., I'll teach you a few Twitter survival tricks.

Abby_Donovan: What makes you think I have nothing better to do with my time than take Twitter 101 lessons from a serial killer?

MarkBaynard: Because somebody peed on you today while you were wearing a Biff the Bunny costume?

Abby_Donovan: Sigh…point taken.

MarkBaynard: You can click on my Profile and hit the FOLLOW button if you want to Follow me.

Abby_Donovan: And just why would I want to Follow you?

MarkBaynard: Because I make really tasty Kool-Aid?

Abby_Donovan: So if I do Follow you, does that mean we're going steady?

MarkBaynard: It's more like a quickie in the back of a cab where we trade fake cell phone numbers afterward.

Abby_Donovan: That would be the longest (and most meaningful) relationship I've had in quite a while.

Abby refreshed the screen four times but there was still no reply. She was wondering if her last post had made her sound too pathetic when the words *"Me too"* appeared on the screen.

A smile touched her lips. *"It was nice meeting you, Mark."*

"It was good for me too," he replied. *"Now if you'll excuse me, I have to go smoke a cigarette and brag to my buddies."*

"Or at least unlock the basement door for your mom."

Then he was gone and she was left staring at the empty box he had left behind. She slid the cursor down to his last entry and clicked on his profile pic. According to his Twitter profile, his name was Mark Baynard, his location was *Wish You Were Here* and he didn't have a website. His bio consisted of three simple words: *Dreamer in Exile.*

Most people floating around in cyberspace seemed to delight in blurting out even the most intimate details of their lives to complete strangers, including the GPS directions to their kid's grade school and the results of their latest colonoscopy. But it seemed Mr. Baynard was perfectly content to remain a man of mystery.

She started to do a Google search on his name but stopped with her fingers poised over the keys. Did she really want to spoil the memory of their silly little flirtation by finding out he wasn't an English lit professor after all, but some sweaty, thick-necked hedge fund manager with three kids, two mortgages, and at least one ex-wife?

According to the stats listed beside his profile pic, he was Following forty-three people and had thirty-two Followers of his own. Abby's cursor hovered over the Follow icon. She didn't suppose there could be any harm in accepting his invitation. According to Hillary, she was on Twitter to establish a rapport with her readers. And every person she met was a potential reader, right?

Making up her mind, she gave the mouse a decisive click. She was now an official Follower of MarkBaynard. She logged off and closed the laptop, shaking her head at her own silliness.

By Monday afternoon she probably would have forgotten all about him. Despite what she might have led him to believe, she had more important things to do with her time than waste it sparring with some snarky stranger on some silly social networking site. Like finishing Chapter Five of her novel in progress.

Chapter Three

*M*arkBaynard: So what are you wearing?

Abby_Donovan: Coffee-stained sweats and the hat Audrey Hepburn wore to the races in MY FAIR LADY. You?

MarkBaynard: Cary Grant's tuxedo from IN-DISCREET and the rubber Ronald Reagan mask Patrick Swayze wore in POINT BREAK.

Abby_Donovan: I'm crushed. I was so hoping for Lyndon Johnson.

MarkBaynard: Are you ready for your first Twitter 101 lesson?

Abby_Donovan: I've already fired up Van Halen's "Hot for Teacher" on my iPod.

MarkBaynard: Okay, the first thing you need to do is download one of the free browser apps like Tweetdeck or Tweetie to help you manage Twitter.

Abby_Donovan: Is it that unruly? Should I also invest in a whip and a chair?

MarkBaynard: Only if you get a leather corset and a pair of thigh-high boots to go along with them.

Abby_Donovan: Has anyone ever told you that you think about sex way too much?

MarkBaynard: Only the stripper sitting on my lap.

Abby_Donovan: So why is Twitter something that needs to be "managed"?

MarkBaynard: It's for organization. So you can split your most important incoming tweets into columns labeled...for instance...MARK BAYNARD.

Abby_Donovan: Or PEOPLE WHO AREN'T MARK BAYNARD.

MarkBaynard: Ouch! With a tongue like that, you won't be needing that whip. You can also have columns for your personal friends and your readers.

Abby_Donovan: Or PEOPLE WHO HAVE ACTUALLY HEARD OF ABIGAIL DONOVAN?

MarkBaynard: I'm guessing THE GRUDGE is one of your favorite films.

Abby_Donovan: Right after THELMA AND LOUISE and BRIEF INTERVIEWS WITH HID-

EOUS MEN. So will this app make posting my twits any easier?

MarkBaynard: Wince! You don't "twit." You "tweet."

Abby_Donovan: Well, pardon me for being such an ignorant twit. Or would that be an ignorant tweet?

MarkBaynard: Sigh...calling a tweet a "twit" is like ordering a "large" drink at Starbucks instead of a "Venti." Your street cred may never recover.

Abby_Donovan: I'm a middle-class white girl who grew up on various army bases. My only street cred consists of downloading BABY GOT BACK for my iPod.

MarkBaynard: Well, you're still pretty fly for a white chick. Which reminds me—you can also download Twitter for your CrackBerry or your iPhone.

Abby_Donovan: Um...what if I don't have a BlackBerry or iPhone?

MarkBaynard: Where do you live? In a cave? Can you see Russia from your house?

Abby_Donovan: No, but I can see some homeless guy urinating behind a bench in Central Park from my apartment window.

MarkBaynard: The same bench you've apparently been sleeping on for the last three years? WITHOUT a BlackBerry or an iPhone?

Abby_Donovan: Why would I need a smart phone? I'm a writer. Other than the daily emergency dash 2 Starbucks, it's not as if I ever leave my apartment.

MarkBaynard: If you did leave your apartment, an app would also make it possible for you to add photos of your travels to your tweets.

Abby_Donovan: You want to see a pic of the homeless guy urinating behind the bench?

MarkBaynard: This might be a good time to remind you that your Followers can see everything you say.

Abby_Donovan: Um...maybe you should have mentioned that 3 twits—I mean 3 tweets—ago.

MarkBaynard: And on the off chance that someone happens to be Following both of us, they'll see our entire conversation.

Abby_Donovan: Don't they have anything better to do? Like watch ROCK OF LOVE: TOUR BUS or KEEPING UP WITH THE KARDASHIANS?

MarkBaynard: If you want to take our conversation private, just hit the Direct Message button.

Abby_Donovan: Like...THIS?

MarkBaynard: That's it. Now we're both flying

under the radar. On some apps like Tweetdeck, Direct messages will have an uppercase "D" in front of them.

Abby_Donovan: I'm glad you told me that. I would have just assumed you were being an even bigger dick than usual.

MarkBaynard: Is that even possible?

Abby_Donovan: Now that you mention it...

MarkBaynard: You also need to beware the Spam Bots.

Abby_Donovan: Are they like the FemBots in the Austin Powers movies? Do they fire bullets from their bosoms?

MarkBaynard: Try to think of them as malevolent R2D2s. If you mention a specific product in your tweets, they'll immediately start Following you.

Abby_Donovan: Is that why @mrsbutterworths is Following me? Because I tweeted that I made myself pancakes for breakfast this morning?

MarkBaynard: Probably. But you should be able to outrun her because I don't think she has any feet.

Abby_Donovan: I don't want to outrun her. I like hearing her voice in my head. It's all warm and syrupy and delicious.

MarkBaynard: And now the most important

part of our lesson: There are two words you must never say on Twitter.

Abby_Donovan: Aunt Jemima?

MarkBaynard: Those two words are…Br*tney Spe*rs. Henceforth to be known as She-Who-Must-Not-Be-Mentioned.

Abby_Donovan: What happens if I forget and mention her?

MarkBaynard: You'll be Followed by a Ukranian spammer whose profile pic is a photoshopped Br*tney performing an act still illegal in many states.

Abby_Donovan: Is there a donkey involved?

MarkBaynard: I didn't say it was illegal in Tijuana.

Abby_Donovan: So what should I do if the naughty Spam Bots track me down?

MarkBaynard: There's a wonderful little feature under Profile called the BLOCK button. Hit it &…poof! That Follower disappears from your life forever.

Abby_Donovan: Sigh…wouldn't it be wonderful if you could Block people in real life?

MarkBaynard: The teenager in front of you driving, combing her hair and texting her BFF at the same time.

Abby_Donovan: The barista who puts whipped

cream on your frappuccino when you order a "Lite."

MarkBaynard: Your funny uncle who drank too much and hugged too hard. Wait...did I say that out loud?

Abby_Donovan: So if you tick me off at any time, I can just Block you and make you disappear. Poof!

MarkBaynard: Or you could simply Unfollow me, which means you wouldn't see my tweets anymore, but I'd be left to pine longingly over yours.

Abby_Donovan: "I'm sorry, Uncle Bobby. You can keep talking but I can't hear you anymore because I Unfollowed you."

MarkBaynard: Who told you my uncle's name was Bobby?

Abby_Donovan: Your therapist.

MarkBaynard: #TherapistFail. Pay attention, Grasshopper. Now I will teach about the FAIL hashtag.

Abby_Donovan: What's a hashtag? It sounds like something you'd eat with ham and eggs.

MarkBaynard: This is the legendary hashtag—#. Add FAIL to it & topple empires. (Or at least deeply embarrass the dry cleaner who lost your best suit.)

Abby_Donovan: Example please?

MarkBaynard: Like #EnronFail

Abby_Donovan: Hmmm...or #TitanicFail?

MarkBaynard: Or #NewCokeFail

Abby_Donovan: Or #AnyMovieStarringPauly Shore(ExceptEncinoManBecauseItAlsoStarred BrendanFraserAndSeanAstin)Fail?

MarkBaynard: Or #MyFirstMarriageFail

Abby_Donovan: I'm afraid to ask about your 2nd, 3rd, and 4th marriages.

MarkBaynard: As long as Wives 2, 3, & 4 don't run into each other at the supermarket, I think it'll be a #Win for all four of us.

Abby_Donovan: Isn't microblogging just thinking out loud? What happens if I can't finish a thought in 140 characters or less?

MarkBaynard: Then you're not clever or pithy enough to be on Twitter and you should go running back to Facebook to fertilize some imaginary crops.

Abby_Donovan: Oh, I can be very pithy. Especially at certain times of the month. Oh wait...you said pithy, didn't you?

MarkBaynard: If you simply can't resist the temptation to drone on and on, boring everyone within tweetshot to distraction, you can always use "..."

MarkBaynard:...which means your Followers

should continue to hang on your every word, no matter how tiresome, self-important or annoying because...

MarkBaynard:...you're not done droning on and on about yourself and your exceedingly dull, pancake-laden, dumb-cell-phone-toting life quite...

MarkBaynard:...yet.

MarkBaynard: BUT you must never forget the cardinal rule of Twitter—If you can't say it in 140 characters, it's probably not worth saying.

Abby_Donovan: Ah, Twitter! Haiku for the semi-literate!

MarkBaynard: That's all for today, Grasshopper. I'm sorry, but I have to go now.

Abby_Donovan: Did Commissioner Gordon just turn on the Bat-Signal?

MarkBaynard: Something like that. Tune in tomorrow. Same Bat-Time. Same Bat-Channel.

Abby_Donovan: Hooked on TV Land, are we?

MarkBaynard: Nick at Nite was always my poison as a kid.

Abby_Donovan: Goodnight John-Boy

MarkBaynard: Goodnight Mary Ellen

Abby_Donovan: Goodnight Daddy

MarkBaynard: Goodnight Erin

Abby_Donovan: Goodnight Jason

MarkBaynard: Goodnight Elizabeth

Abby_Donovan: Goodnight Ben

MarkBaynard: Goodnight Grandma

Abby_Donovan: Goodnight Jim-Bob

MarkBaynard: Goodnight Tweetheart...

Tuesday, April 26—3:00 P.M.

MarkBaynard: What are you wearing?

Abby_Donovan: Coffee-stained sweats and the jaunty beret Faye Dunaway wore in BONNIE AND CLYDE. You?

MarkBaynard: Ricardo Montalban's fake chest from STAR TREK 2: THE WRATH OF KHAN and Arnold Schwarzenegger's shades from TER-MINATOR.

Abby_Donovan: I knew you'd be back!

MarkBaynard: How could I resist? I just had to know how my star Twitter pupil was doing.

Abby_Donovan: You're going to be so proud of me! I downloaded Tweetdeck and learned how to post a pic. http://tweetpic.com/28251900

MarkBaynard: What in the hell is that? A dust-mop?

Abby_Donovan: That's my cat Buffy the Mouse Slayer.

MarkBaynard: I naturally assumed your cat's name would be Pebbles.

Abby_Donovan: I actually have two cats.

MarkBaynard: You should do a head count. Maybe Buffy ate the other cat.

Abby_Donovan: Nope. Willow Tum-Tum is sitting right here in my lap, purring and gazing up at me in drunken adoration. http://tweetpic .com/282519061

MarkBaynard: I used to do that to my wife until she took out the restraining order.

Abby_Donovan: Willow lawyered up and got mine overturned. I knew I shouldn't have let her watch so much LAW & ORDER as a kitten.

MarkBaynard: So is Willow Tum-Tum the secret love child of Biff the Bunny & Henry/Henrietta Hedgehog?

Abby_Donovan: Her name was just Willow, but she loves to have her stomach rubbed so that devolved into an embarrassing ritual called "Tum-Tum Alert!"

MarkBaynard: Embarrassing for you or for her?

Abby_Donovan: Both. Willow Tum-Tum isn't the only one who adores me. Did you notice I picked up another 42 Followers today?

MarkBaynard: Or as you probably prefer to think of them—fawning sycophants.

Abby_Donovan: Or "people with impeccable taste who have actually read and loved my book."

MarkBaynard: Ouch! You're relentless, woman! I promise to download it to my e-reader as soon as I finish the new Paris Hilton autobiography.

Abby_Donovan: Don't.

MarkBaynard: Now you're just being a tease.

Abby_Donovan: No. I'm serious. I don't want you to read it. I don't even want you to go to my website.

MarkBaynard: Why not? Too many pics of your head photoshopped onto Angelina Jolie's naked body?

Abby_Donovan: For the past 4 years, the only reason anyone has wanted to talk to me is because I'm "Abigail Donovan, the author."

MarkBaynard: As opposed to "Abigail Donovan, the Luddite with no iPhone or BlackBerry"?

Abby_Donovan: What I'm trying to say is that it's kind of nice to have someone talk to me because I'm me. Just Abby.

MarkBaynard: And Willow Tum-Tum's mommy.

Abby_Donovan: Don't forget Buffy the Mouse Slayer. She's very sensitive and she's listening.

MarkBaynard: Yeah, I wouldn't want her to eat me.

Abby_Donovan: So I've sent you a pic. Why don't you send me one?

MarkBaynard: I don't have a cat.

Abby_Donovan: I can see that you're tweeting from your iPhone today. Why don't you send me a pic of what you're looking at this very moment?

MarkBaynard: Sure. Hang on…give me a minute.

MarkBaynard: Okay…you still there? Here's the view from where I'm sitting. http://twitphoto .com/MB7sta

MarkBaynard: Abby?

MarkBaynard: Abby, are you still there?

Abby_Donovan: Um, Mark…that's the Eiffel Tower. Are you in Las Vegas at the Paris casino by any chance?

MarkBaynard: Not exactly.

Abby_Donovan: You're in Paris? You've been in Paris all this time??? PARIS FREAKING FRANCE???

MarkBaynard: I told you I was an English lit professor on sabbatical traveling the world and writing the Mediocre American Novel.

Abby_Donovan: I thought you were kidding about the traveling the world part.

MarkBaynard: Didn't I sound serious?

Abby_Donovan: You never sound serious.

MarkBaynard: It's a curse I share with David Letterman, Groucho Marx, and George W. Bush.

Abby_Donovan: Wistful sigh...I've always wanted to go to Paris. Tell me exactly what you're doing at this very moment.

MarkBaynard: Sending you a tweet.

Abby_Donovan: You know what I mean!

MarkBaynard: Sitting outside a cafe called Boulangerie Patisserie, sipping a tiny cup of espresso so dark and thick I won't sleep for a week.

Abby_Donovan: Oh, I can almost taste the bitterness of the coffee grounds on my tongue!

MarkBaynard: I'm also watching exceedingly thin women in desperate need of a Supersized Big Mac Combo Meal parade past on the busy sidewalk.

Abby_Donovan: Oh, I can almost feel the hunger pangs of the women!

MarkBaynard: If I light a cigarette, will it make you cough?

Abby_Donovan: Do you smoke?

MarkBaynard: No. But it's never too late to start. Especially when you're in France.

Abby_Donovan: How long will you be there? In Paris Freaking France?

MarkBaynard: Only one more day. I'm leaving for the Loire Valley tomorrow.

Abby_Donovan: Moan...the Loire Valley? Where they keep the chauteaux and the wine?

MarkBaynard: I'll be traveling through the Loire Valley for a week or two, then on to Tuscany and Florence.

Abbey: Florence, Italy?!

MarkBaynard: Florence, Alabama. But seriously (I said that so you'd know I was being serious), I'm spending time in Italy before heading for Ireland.

Abby_Donovan: Sob! I'm going to Starbucks tomorrow. Then on to the gym and the dry cleaner.

MarkBaynard: Will you send me a pic from there?

Abby_Donovan: Yes. I'll be the blue woman with the plastic bag wrapped around her head.

MarkBaynard: Is this a bad time to ask you how the writing went today?

Abby_Donovan: Pretty much the same way it went yesterday. I'm still stuck on Chapter Five.

MarkBaynard: If you won't let me read your first book, you can at least tell me about it.

Abby_Donovan: Not much to tell. It was called TIME OUT OF MIND. It's a novel about a young girl growing up with a bipolar mother.

MarkBaynard: A comedy, eh?

Abby_Donovan: I like to think it made the readers laugh & cry.

MarkBaynard: Tell me the first sentence.

Abby_Donovan: You think I'm egotistical enough to have the first sentence of my first book memorized?

MarkBaynard: You're a writer, aren't you?

Abby_Donovan: "Even as a girl my mom had a crooked smile, as if she couldn't quite decide whether she wanted to be manic or depressive."

Abby_Donovan: Mark? Did you doze off?

MarkBaynard: I thought you said the book was a novel, not a memoir.

Abby_Donovan: How did you know I wrote that about my own mom?

MarkBaynard: Built-in bullshit detector. Only it works the opposite way. I can tell when someone is pretending to lie.

Abby_Donovan: Well, there are elements of truth in all great fiction, don't you think?

MarkBaynard: And elements of fiction in all great truths. Is your mom still alive?

Abby_Donovan: Nursing home. Bipolar+ Dementia=#MedicationFail. I moved her to a wonderful facility in the Bronx 2 years ago after we lost my dad.

MarkBaynard: So very sorry. Were you a daddy's girl?

Abby_Donovan: He was always my rock. My security. Since he's been gone, the world seems like a much bigger, much scarier place.

MarkBaynard: When you were a kid, did you ever worry that you would get sick like your mom?

Abby_Donovan: Daddy always told me not to worry about that. That I was cursed with his face but blessed with his brain...

Abby_Donovan: But I was still pretty relieved when I realized the voices I'd been hearing in my head belonged to my characters.

MarkBaynard: Does your mom still recognize you?

Abby_Donovan: Most of the time. On the days she doesn't, I'm not sure I recognize myself either.

MarkBaynard: Believe me...there are days when I wish my mother didn't recognize me. Hang on...oh crap!

Abby_Donovan: What is it?

MarkBaynard: One of the anorexic Frenchwomen was just blown away by a stray gust of wind. I'd better go see if I can catch her.

Abby_Donovan: Goodnight Principal Snyder

MarkBaynard: Goodnight Darla

Abby_Donovan: Goodnight Oz

MarkBaynard: Goodnight Tara

Abby_Donovan: Goodnight Xander

MarkBaynard: Goodnight Drusilla

Abby_Donovan: Goodnight Spike

MarkBaynard: Goodnight Buffy

Abby_Donovan: Goodnight Angel

MarkBaynard: Goodnight Tweetheart...

Tuesday, May 3—2:39 P.M.

MarkBaynard: What are you wearing?

Abby_Donovan: Coffee-stained sweats and Hermione Granger's Hogwarts scarf. You?

MarkBaynard: Samuel L. Jackson's Jheri curls from PULP FICTION and Frank-N-Furter's corset from ROCKY HORROR PICTURE SHOW.

Abby_Donovan: Have you made it to the Loire Valley yet? You promised me a pic so I could live vicariously through you.

MarkBaynard: VIEW FROM MY iPHONE: http://twitphoto.com/MB7stb

Abby_Donovan: Sigh...it's the Chateau de Villandry, isn't it? Tell me EXACTLY what you're doing at this very moment.

MarkBaynard: Sitting beneath a vine-covered

pergola, nibbling on sun-warmed goat cheese & admiring a re-creation of a medieval herb garden.

Abby_Donovan: Did I tell you I had some Velveeta today? I took a pic of my view for you too...

Abby_Donovan: VIEW FROM MY LAPTOP: http://tweetpic.com/282519064

MarkBaynard: Is that a Gollum doll climbing over the back of your computer? I'm guessing it hasn't been a very productive writing day, my pre-ciousssss.

Abby_Donovan: Let's just put it this way—I know why Hemingway shot himself.

MarkBaynard: So do I. Because he couldn't drink himself to death fast enough.

Abby_Donovan: Every day I tell myself that this is the day I'm going to finish Chapter Five and start Chapter Six.

MarkBaynard: Maybe you're being too hard on yourself. It can't be that bad. When is the book due?

Abby_Donovan: March of 2009.

MarkBaynard: But this is May of...oh...never mind...

Abby_Donovan: So far Chapter Five consists solely of "All work and no play makes Abby a dull girl" written 6000 times.

MarkBaynard: Please tell me you don't own an ax.

Abby_Donovan: No, but I did see some spooky twins hanging around the elevator yesterday.

MarkBaynard: Maybe you're just suffering from imposter syndrome.

Abby_Donovan: Shouldn't that be your gig? Especially if you really are Ashton Kutcher. Or Batman.

MarkBaynard: I've read it happens to people who experience "overnight" success but secretly believe they don't deserve it.

Abby_Donovan: Let me guess. You minored in psychology.

MarkBaynard: Actually it was a double major. I minored in pissing people off.

Abby_Donovan: I bet you graduated at the top of your class.

MarkBaynard: Summa Cum Laude all the way, babe.

Abby_Donovan: I haven't really felt like an imposter since the book hit so big. More like a guest star in my own life.

MarkBaynard: The part of Abigail Donovan is now being played by Tina Fey.

Abby_Donovan: Only because that chick who played Nellie Olesen on LITTLE HOUSE ON THE PRAIRIE wasn't available.

MarkBaynard: At least you've made it to Chapter Five of your second book. I haven't even made it to Chapter One of my first book yet.

Abby_Donovan: You should be grateful you're not published yet. No deadlines. No expectations. No crippling fear you'll disappoint everyone who matters.

MarkBaynard: No fortune. No fame. No adoring sycophants.

Abby_Donovan: Don't make me Block you. I already had to Block several people today.

MarkBaynard: Why?

Abby_Donovan: I tweeted a joke about my "ginormous freak feet" and the panty hose fetishists started following me.

MarkBaynard: Friend with pet squirrel mentioned being a "squirrel lover" w/equally shocking results. There really IS something for everybody on Twitter.

Abby_Donovan: I'm thinking of starting a new hashtag. #How2LoseFollowers.

MarkBaynard: #How2LoseFollowers: Insult the president. Any president. Obama. Bush. Clinton. George Washington. It doesn't matter.

Abby_Donovan: #How2LoseFollowers: Describe in graphic detail just how long it's been since you last shaved yr legs.

MarkBaynard: #How2LoseFollowers: Tweet any recipe including cabbage and calf brains.

Abby_Donovan: #How2LoseFollowers: Make snarky comments about Sarah Palin's hair and/or the president's ears.

MarkBaynard: #How2LoseFollowers: Choose pic of Kim Jong-il as your avatar. Or Kathie Lee Gifford.

Abby_Donovan: #How2LoseFollowers: Tweet link to URL citing potential health hazards of binging on dark chocolate M&M's.

MarkBaynard: #How2LoseFollowers: Tweet that you think COLD MOUNTAIN had the best ending EVER!

Abby_Donovan: #How2LoseFollowers: Tell me you bet I have really pretty toes and you'd like to hook up.

MarkBaynard: I bet you have really pretty toes. Wanna hook up?

Abby_Donovan: Hang on...let me wiggle into my panty hose and I'll get back to you.

MarkBaynard: Fortunately, Twitter isn't eHarmony. People may come here looking for feet, but they don't come here looking for love.

Abby_Donovan: Don't be silly. People never stop looking for love.

MarkBaynard: Yeah, some of them don't even stop AFTER they've found it.

Abby_Donovan: A cynic, are we?

MarkBaynard: No, just a divorced realist.

Abby_Donovan: You give new meaning to the phrase "hopeless romantic," don't you?

MarkBaynard: My wife may not be Following me anymore but what about you? Is there anything I could do to make you Unfollow me?

Abby_Donovan: You could tell me who you voted for in the last election.

MarkBaynard: Who told you about that life-size cardboard cutout of Hillary Clinton I keep in the corner of my bedroom?

Abby_Donovan: My NRA poster of Dick Cheney is MUCH sexier. I never could resist a guy with a big gun.

MarkBaynard: You know we liberal guys are all secretly hot for Ann Coulter.

Abby_Donovan: Yeah, I bet you get hot just thinking about her bony little elbows digging into your groin.

MarkBaynard: Well, we've gotten the taboo topic of politics out of the way. What's next? Religion?

Abby_Donovan: Why not? Do you believe in God?

MarkBaynard: Oddly enough, he may be the only thing I ever really did believe in.

Abby_Donovan: And you have the nerve to call yourself a cynic!

MarkBaynard: No, I said I was a realist. So if God is real...

Abby_Donovan: I wish I had your confidence.

MarkBaynard: So let me get this straight—I'm a God-fearing Liberal and you're a Conservative Atheist?

Abby_Donovan: I never said I was an atheist. I prefer to think of myself as a devout Narcissist.

MarkBaynard: What does that mean?

Abby_Donovan: If the sun is shining, I thank God. If it rains, I blame him.

MarkBaynard: I think that just makes you a human being. Damn. There goes the Bat-Signal again. Must be another old lady's cat stuck in a tree.

Abby_Donovan: Goodnight Deputy Leo

MarkBaynard: Goodnight Lilly

Abby_Donovan: Goodnight Wallace

MarkBaynard: Goodnight Mac

Abby_Donovan: Goodnight Logan

MarkBaynard: Goodnight Kendall

Abby_Donovan: Goodnight Keith

MarkBaynard: Goodnight Backup

Abby_Donovan: Will you marry me?

MarkBaynard: Why?

Abby_Donovan: Because I made a vow that I'd marry the first man who knew the name of Veronica Mars's dog.

MarkBaynard: Tell you what—if neither one of us has found anyone to marry by the time I turn 15, it's a deal.

Abby_Donovan: I just hope you like older women.

MarkBaynard: Oh, I do. Goodnight Tweetheart...

Chapter Four

MarkBaynard: What are you wearing?

    Abby_Donovan: Coffee-stained sweats and Madeline Kahn's hairdo after the monster made love to her in YOUNG FRANKENSTEIN. You?

MarkBaynard: Keanu Reeves's long black duster from THE MATRIX and Harry Shearer's leather pants from THIS IS SPINAL TAP.

Abby_Donovan: The ones with the foil-wrapped cucumber in them?

MarkBaynard: I'll never tell. Let's just say it was hell getting through airport security this morning.

Abby_Donovan: Ah…another airport, another glamorous city! So where in the world is Mark Baynard today?

MarkBaynard: VIEW FROM MY iPHONE: http://twitphoto.com/MB7stc

Abby_Donovan: Wistful sigh...Ah, Tuscany! 'Fess up. Tell me what you're doing at this very minute.

MarkBaynard: Sipping a lush Merlot on the balcony of a villa overlooking the vineyards. You?

Abby_Donovan: VIEW FROM MY LAPTOP: http://tweetpic.com/282519066

MarkBaynard: Is that Captain Jack Sparrow hisself peeking over the back of your computer? Avast ye matey! Have I missed Talk Like a Pirate Day?

Abby_Donovan: When I get discouraged my Captain Jack doll swaggers onto my desk and mumbles sweet nothings in my ear to inspire me.

MarkBaynard: I thought that was my job. So what have you written today?

Abby_Donovan: 2 blogs, 7 Facebook updates & 18 tweets. Oh, & a check to the cable company. You would have been stunned by my eloquence on the MEMO line.

MarkBaynard: If all else fails, maybe we can publish our tweets and pass them off as a collaboration.

Abby_Donovan: Only if the police don't seize them as evidence after they search your refrigerator.

MarkBaynard: I'll print them out and hide

them behind the bottle of Chianti. Next to the fava beans.

Abby_Donovan: They might need a mug shot for AMERICA'S MOST WANTED too. Why don't you send me a pic with you actually IN it?

MarkBaynard: You HAVE sent me naked pictures of your cats. Maybe it is time we exchanged pics. Clothing optional, of course. At least for you.

Abby_Donovan: I guess that means the Catholic schoolgirl uniform is a no-go.

MarkBaynard: Whoa! Let's not be too hasty.

Abby_Donovan: Meet me back here in 15 minutes. We'll synchronize our watches, count down from 10, and push the UPLOAD button at the exact same nanosecond.

MarkBaynard: It's a date.

Monday, May 9—2:10 P.M.

MarkBaynard: Are you sure you're ready for this?

Abby_Donovan: I was born ready, baby. Deep breath. Ten...

MarkBaynard: Nine...

Abby_Donovan: Eight...

MarkBaynard: Seven...

Abby_Donovan: Six…

MarkBaynard: Five…

Abby_Donovan: Four…

MarkBaynard: Three…

Abby_Donovan: Two…

MarkBaynard: NOW!!!

MarkBaynard: http://twitphoto.com/MB7ste

Abby_Donovan:http://tweetpic.com/282519068

MarkBaynard: That's odd. You're a dead ringer for Angelina Jolie in that pic. You even have the same tattoos.

Abby_Donovan: And you are the spitting image of Brad Pitt. When did you get your pic snapped on the red carpet at the Oscars?

MarkBaynard: If you want to know the truth, I'm crushed. I was hoping you looked a lot more like Jennifer Aniston.

Abby_Donovan: And I was hoping you looked a lot more like David Schwimmer.

MarkBaynard: So…now that we've exchanged fake pics, it's confirmed that we're both in the Witness Protection Program.

Abby_Donovan: Or we're both craven cowards with intimacy issues.

MarkBaynard: Don't be ridiculous. I can be very intimate. Sometimes I even call my students by their first names.

Abby_Donovan: Everybody is so transparent these days but always in a very superficial way. Is it so wrong to want to preserve a little mystery in life?

MarkBaynard: Not if you're in the Witness Protection Program.

Abby_Donovan: Besides, I sort of like it this way. I can change your appearance based on my mood. Monday you might be Gerard Butler. Tuesday, Clive Owen...

MarkBaynard: And I can change your outfit according to mine. Monday you could be a Catholic schoolgirl. Tuesday a naughty nurse...

Abby_Donovan: What? No leather-clad, whip-toting dominatrix?

MarkBaynard: I'm saving her for Saturday night. Especially if I've been a very naughty boy that week.

Abby_Donovan: Shall we make a pact then? I won't go looking for your pic online if you won't go looking for mine.

MarkBaynard: You're on. You shall remain a woman of mystery in a French maid costume and stiletto heels.

Abby_Donovan: And you shall remain Hugh Jackman, Jude Law, Matthew McConaughey, Viggo Mortensen, Sawyer from LOST and/or Sean Astin.

MarkBaynard: Sean Astin? Samwise Gamgee???

Abby_Donovan: Don't you be dissin' my plump little hobbit love muffin!

MarkBaynard: I had you pegged as more of a Frodo woman.

Abby_Donovan: Ha! Frodo was adorable but he couldn't have found his ass with both hands without his loyal Samwise to help him.

MarkBaynard: Even I have to admit it was a classic bromance.

Abby_Donovan: I love that moment toward the end of the movie when Frodo wakes up & realizes he's alive & Sam appears in the doorway & looks at him...

Abby_Donovan:... as if to say, "I will always be your friend. I will always love you no matter what you've done & no matter what you'll ever do."

MarkBaynard: "Even if that includes trying to hog up the ring of power for yourself and almost destroying the world, you greedy little bugger.".

Abby_Donovan: I've always thought it would be lovely to have someone look at me that way. Besides Willow Tum-Tum, of course.

MarkBaynard: What about Buffy the Mouse Slayer? Doesn't she look at you that way too?

Abby_Donovan: No, she looks at me as if to say,

"If you were smaller, I know I could find a way to eat you."

MarkBaynard: Now that we've determined which hobbit you'd most like to perv on, it might be time to take the next step in our relationship.

Abby_Donovan: Do I have to meet your parents?

MarkBaynard: I don't even want to meet my parents. Not for lunch. Not for coffee. Not for Thanksgiving.

Abby_Donovan: They sound like charming people.

MarkBaynard: Oh, they are. Sort of a cross between the Clampetts and the Borgias.

Abby_Donovan: Do you have any brothers or sisters?

MarkBaynard: I have a little sister who adores me and an older brother who doesn't.

Abby_Donovan: Why? Did Mommy always love you best?

MarkBaynard: No, she loved me least. Except when she was drinking. Then she loved everybody. Especially the mailman, to whom I bear a marked resemblance.

Abby_Donovan: As an only child whose siblings were strictly imaginary, I'm always fascinated by family dynamics.

MarkBaynard: Trust me—sometimes imaginary is better. Of course sometimes inflatable is better too.

Abby_Donovan: There you go again. Using humor as a defense mechanism.

MarkBaynard: I figured out in the first grade that it was better to crack a joke than somebody's skull.

Abby_Donovan: It might just be your way of keeping people at arm's length.

MarkBaynard: Did I tell you the one about the daughter of the bipolar and the son of the drunk who walk into a bar together?

Abby_Donovan: No, but I'm guessing one of them has a talking dog.

MarkBaynard: And a mute, one-legged parrot.

Abby_Donovan: So if I don't get to meet your parents (or your parrot), then what IS the next step in our relationship?

MarkBaynard: I'm kind of an old-fashioned guy so I thought I'd ask you out on a date before begging you to tweet me a topless photo.

Abby_Donovan: A date? Won't that be a challenge since we're on different...you know...continents?

MarkBaynard: No challenge is too great for

Twitter. Just be in front of your computer on Friday night at 7 p.m. and I'll pick you up.

Abby_Donovan: You're assuming I don't have anything better to do on Friday night at 7 p.m. than have an imaginary date with a man I've never even met.

MarkBaynard: Do you?

Abby_Donovan: No.

MarkBaynard: Good.

Abby_Donovan: We're in different time zones. Won't that be after midnight for you?

MarkBaynard: I don't mind. I'm a notoriously lousy sleeper.

Abby_Donovan: 7 p.m. it is, then. I'll be waiting for you. Um...what should I wear? Casual or formal?

MarkBaynard: Surprise me. (Although I'm hoping you haven't completely ruled out the Catholic schoolgirl outfit.)

Abby_Donovan: Goodnight Lorelai

Abby_Donovan: Mark? Are you still there?

Abby_Donovan: Did I do it? DID I DO IT???!!! Did I stump you?!

MarkBaynard: I'm just afraid if I admit I watched GILMORE GIRLS you'll think I'm gay instead of just an insomniac who watches too much TV.

Abby_Donovan: Since we've been talking Witness Protection, how about Goodnight Uncle Junior?

MarkBaynard: Goodnight Carmela

Abby_Donovan: Goodnight Tony

MarkBaynard: Goodnight Meadow

Abby_Donovan: Goodnight Silvio

MarkBaynard: Goodnight Adriana

Abby_Donovan: Goodnight Big...um...Goodnight Salvatore

MarkBaynard: Goodnight Tweetheart...

"Goodnight, Tweetheart," Abby whispered, putting her MacBook to sleep with a stroke of her fingertip.

Her hands lingered over the keyboard. Despite the smoky warmth of Steve Tyrell's voice crooning "For All We Know" from her iPod dock speakers, she suddenly felt very alone. How could Mark be halfway across the world when she would have sworn he'd been in this room with her only seconds ago?

She dragged her eyes away from the computer screen to gaze out the window. While she had been tweeting, the clouds that had been hanging over the city since early that morning had finally decided to deliver on their promise of rain. On Fifth

Avenue far below, brightly colored umbrellas were springing open like something out of a child's pop-up book. Twilight was still hours away, but the cabbies had flicked on their headlights, bathing the slick streets converging on Grand Army Plaza in a shimmering wash of silver. On the far side of the plaza, the wind tossed the tender green leaves crowning the park's ancient oaks.

In spite of the melancholy gloom of the afternoon, Abby could almost feel the seductive warmth of the sun against her face. Could almost see herself standing on a stone terrace with vineyards stretched out below her as far as the eye could see. Could almost smell the ripening grapes hanging lush and heavy on the vines.

She turned, her floral sundress rippling around her ankles, only to find a man standing at the edge of the terrace. Though his face was in shadow, she somehow knew he was smiling and that his smile held the unspoken promise that she would never again be as lonely as she had been before she turned to find him standing there.

Willow Tum-Tum bounded into her lap, jerking Abby out of her ridiculous daydream. Sighing, she stroked her fingers through Willow's thick, soft ruff, coaxing an adoring purr from the cat's throat. If she didn't rein in her imagination soon, she was going to have to turn her hand to writing the romance novels she secretly loved to read in the bathtub.

She should have never let herself be drawn into this situation. Wasn't social media notorious for establishing a sense of false intimacy? How else to explain the way she'd been blurting out intimate details about her life, her career, and her past to a man she'd never met, a man she probably never *would* meet?

She wouldn't have dared tell her editor about the fear that paralyzed her every time she sat down at her computer to finish Chapter Five of her new book. And no one, not even her best friend, knew how adrift she'd felt since her father died.

Her dad had always been her biggest cheerleader. He might have played the role of big, tough army guy for his troops, but he never missed a chance to help her with her homework or braid her hair before bedtime. If she was in a school play, he was always front and center in the first row of the auditorium, beaming with pride as she lisped out her lines or pirouetted across the stage dressed as Pocahontas or a Thanksgiving pumpkin.

She still remembered calling him late one night when she was writing her book and tearfully telling him she was having trouble with a scene because the heroine's dad in the book was dying and she couldn't bear to write a dead dad scene.

He had thought about it for a minute, then said, "That's okay, honey. Go ahead and finish me off. Everybody's gotta go sometime."

After *Time Out of Mind* had been published, he had loaded down his car trunk with boxes of books and tried to sell a copy to everybody he met. His easygoing charm and pride in his only daughter's accomplishments were so irresistible that he usually ended up selling two.

She picked up the framed photo sitting on the corner of her desk. It was a grainy Polaroid she had taken of her parents in happier times when they probably weren't much older than she was now. They were standing on Carolina Beach against a backdrop of sand and sea. Her dad had one burly arm draped over her mother's shoulders. He was grinning at the camera like a mischievous nine-year-old while her mother laughed up at him, her eyes hidden by a pair of oversize sunglasses and her long brown hair dancing in the wind. The hint of sadness that usually haunted her smile had vanished, if only for the instant it had taken for Abby to freeze that moment in time.

Abby hadn't realized until after her dad's death that there were hardly any pictures of the three of them together. One of them had always been holding the camera. She gently returned the photo to its place, her smile a wistful echo of her mother's.

She supposed this was what came of pouring your heart out to a total stranger. Mooning over old photos while listening to the lonely wail of a saxophone, two cats your only company.

She closed the screen of her laptop with a decisive click. Bantering and "flirting" with Mark through Direct Messages had seemed harmless enough, but making a date to take their relationship to the next level felt more than a little disingenuous.

She glanced at her *Far Side* desk calendar. It was only Monday. She had four days to decide whether or not she was going to make an appearance at the appointed time or stand up her cyberdate in favor of a real man, one who might be able to offer her more than just words on a screen.

She had four days to forget all about Mark Baynard.

Chapter Five

I met a man online."

Abby's announcement might not have been so dramatic if it hadn't been gasped out in what sounded like her dying breath. Fortunately her friend Margo was accustomed to her wheezing so she didn't whip out her BlackBerry and start dialing 911 or leap off her own treadmill and go running for the gym defibrillator.

Using the towel draped around her neck to wipe the sweat from her eyes, Abby glanced down at the treadmill's digital readout. She groaned, finding it hard to believe she'd only been slogging along for seventeen minutes when it felt more like seventeen hours. She much preferred taking a long, leisurely stroll in the park or *Partying Off the Pounds* while Richard Simmons shouted that she was born to be a star. She had always hated to run unless something was chasing her—preferably a hungry bear.

She shot Margo a resentful glance. Margo had

the long, lean muscles and regal posture of an Amazonian queen. She ran with her head straight up, her cocoa-colored eyes fixed on some invisible kingdom she had yet to conquer.

Margo didn't even sweat. She gleamed.

If Abby didn't love her so much, she would have hated her.

"So I met a man online," she repeated. "I know that probably sounds pathetic."

"Not coming from a budding agoraphobic," Margo replied. Although her pace was twice as fast as Abby's and her beautifully toned arms were pumping like a pair of well-oiled pistons, she was still perfectly capable of carrying on a normal conversation, placing a stock order on the headset of her BlackBerry, or singing the opening aria from *La Traviata*. "Unless you're into those guys who deliver Chinese food, where else would you meet a man? You hardly ever leave your apartment except to go to Starbucks and visit your mom in the nursing home."

"Hey! I get out! I met you at the gym here today, didn't I?"

"And how many times have you turned me down for lunch in the past three months?"

"I told you I was sorry about that. I've been extremely busy lately."

Margo cocked one perfectly waxed eyebrow in her direction, her expression more compassionate than snide. "Doing what? Finishing your book?"

Abby felt her throat begin to close up as it did whenever anyone mentioned her work in progress. Or her work *not* in progress. "I'll have you know that I just may be on the verge of my biggest creative breakthrough yet."

"On what? The title page? The dedication?"

"Well, it certainly won't be dedicated to *you* this time," Abby muttered under her breath.

"Look, sugar," Margo drawled, making Abby wince. The sweeter and thicker Margo's Atlanta accent got, the more dangerous she became. She'd been known to make the grown men in her brokerage firm cry simply by sliding a "God love you" or a "bless your little heart" into their annual performance reviews. "I don't mean to be so hard on you, but I'm afraid you're only a few takeout orders away from becoming some crazy cat lady who stays triple dead-bolted in her apartment twenty-four hours a day and bakes poisoned cookies for the children in her building."

"I believe you have to have more than two cats to qualify as a crazy cat lady," Abby replied stiffly. "Forty-two is optimal. And you know I'm a rotten cook so the poisoning will probably be ruled accidental. Besides, if I don't turn something in to my publisher soon, I won't have an apartment. I'll be pushing a shopping cart full of all my worldly belongings—and my cats—around the park."

Margo snorted. "The mayor won't even let you get away with that these days. That's just going to earn you a one-way bus ticket to Boca Raton."

"Sadly enough, that's starting to sound like a perfectly good option. I've heard Boca Raton is lovely this time of year."

Margo slowed her pace to match Abby's—a sign that she'd begun her cooldown. "So just exactly where did you find this guy—www.Escaped Convicts.com?"

"I met him on Twitter," Abby reluctantly admitted.

"Well, that bodes well for a long-term relationship. At least if he dumps you he can do it in one hundred forty characters or less, which is so much better than on a Post-it note."

"Is this a bad time to remind you that we met while speed dating?" Abby asked, referring to the dreaded urban game of musical chairs that involved answering a matchmaking cattle call, then spending three to eight minutes interviewing a potential lifetime mate before moving on to the next prospect.

It was only after she and Margo had drawn their numbers and ended up sitting across a table from each other at a crowded bar in Soho that they had realized it was a gay speed dating service. They had sat gazing awkwardly at each other for over a minute before Abby had blurted out, "I'm afraid I'm not gay. But if I was, I'm sure I'd find you very attractive."

"I'm not gay, either," Margo had confessed, dissolving in husky ripples of laughter. "But if I was, you sure as hell wouldn't be my type. I'd want one of those butch chicks with the tattoos and the mullet."

They'd spent the next eight minutes comparing dating horror stories. When the bell rang, signaling that their time was up, they'd ducked out a fire exit and spent half the night at the Back Fence in Greenwich Village listening to jazz and drinking chocolate martinis.

"Based on how *we* met," Abby said, "our relationship should have only lasted for about seven and a half minutes instead of three years."

"Just what do you know about this guy?"

"His name is Mark . . . I think," she added under her breath. "He's on sabbatical from his job as a college professor. His first marriage ended badly, possibly from adultery—hers, not his. He knows a lot about pop culture and classic TV. Oh, and he doesn't get along with his mom."

"Perfect. He's unemployed, divorced, has mommy issues, and can beat you at Trivial Pursuit because he has nothing better to do all day than sit around and watch TV. I hate to be the one to point this out, but he doesn't exactly sound like a candidate for Mr. Right. Or even Mr. Right Now. Maybe you should consider EscapedConvicts.com after all. You might be able to find some guy with a job, even if it's only working in the prison laundry."

Abby could feel her temper rising. " 'On sabbatical' is not the same thing as unemployed. He's also funny and smart and he makes me laugh—something I haven't felt a whole hell of a lot like doing lately. And I know the Internet can create this false sense of intimacy, but it's still the weirdest thing. It's like I can tell him things I can't tell anybody else. Things I can't even tell—"

"Your best friend?" Margo interjected wryly.

Abby blew out a sheepish sigh. "He even asked me out on a date for this Friday."

"Oooh . . . a tweet-up?" Margo pursed her glossy red lips, actually looking intrigued. "In a public place, I hope . . . with nine-one-one programmed into your speed dial."

"Well . . . it's not exactly a *real* date. I'm supposed to meet him on Twitter Friday night at seven o'clock. He's sort of . . . well . . . in Italy right now."

That confession forced Margo to do the unthinkable. She turned off her treadmill. Before the full forty-five minutes of her workout was over. As the rubber belt slowed to a halt, Abby briefly considered leaping off of her own machine while it was still running and making a desperate dash for the women's locker room. But she knew she wouldn't make it past the row of ellipticals before Margo would be on her like a cheetah on a lame gazelle.

Margo stepped off the treadmill and made a brief show of toweling the nonexistent sweat from her throat and chest, no doubt to make Abby feel marginally better about the steady stream of perspiration still trickling between her own breasts. "Honey, I know you haven't dated a lot of guys since you and Dean broke up, but could you have possibly chosen a more inaccessible man? The only way this guy could be less attainable was if he was still married. Which, for all you know, bless your little heart, he is."

Abby cringed. If Margo followed up her "bless your little heart" with a "God love you," Abby was going to end up bleeding to death all over the floor of the gym.

"Look—Dean dumped me over a year ago. Don't you think it's time I dipped my toe back into the metaphorical pool?"

"Dean might have turned out to be a cheating scumbag, but at least he was real. This guy is like the Old Spice guy but without the towel and horse. He's nothing but a fantasy. An empty Armani suit you can fill with whoever you want him to be."

"Hugh Jackman," Abby murmured, slowing her own pace to a lethargic walk. "Or Samwise Gamgee."

"What?"

Abby shook her head. "Nothing." She sighed, having run out of irrational arguments to counter her friend's perfectly logical concerns. "I haven't even decided whether or not I'm going to show up on Friday night. Maybe I should just let the whole thing drop before it gets out of hand and he wants to start naked Skyping or something."

"Or having tweetsex."

Abby frowned. "Is it even possible to have sex in a hundred and forty characters or less?"

Margo rolled her eyes. "If you'd dated some of the men I have, you'd know it's possible to have sex in one hundred forty *seconds* or less."

"Ah, speed sex instead of speed dating." Abby turned off her own treadmill and joined Margo on the floor. "I wish I could introduce the two of you. I think he'd like you."

Margo slung one lean, sculpted arm around Abby's shoulder as they made their way toward the women's locker room. "Just tell him I'm your obligatory sassy but wise African-American best friend and I'll drop-kick his ass to the moon if he breaks your heart."

"Should I tell him your name is Chantal or Bon Qui Qui? 'Margo' is a little too vanilla, don't you think?"

"Just tell him I'm Oprah to your Gayle."

"Hey, you got to be Oprah last week! It's your turn to be Gayle to my Oprah."

"You can call me whatever you like as long as they get Beyoncé to play me when they make a movie of your life."

"I was thinking more along the lines of Kathy Griffin."

Margo slanted her an evil look, her embrace tightening into a choke hold. "Do it and I'll drop-kick *your* lily-white ass to the moon."

"You're right, God love your little heart. On second thought, maybe RuPaul will be available." Shrugging off her friend's arm, Abby ducked through the locker room door just in time to avoid the deadly snap of Margo's gym towel.

#

Her eyes glued to the Direct Message column on her Tweetdeck, Abby took another nervous sip from the glass of chardonnay perched on the desk next to her MacBook. Given how rapidly it was disappearing, she should have kept the bottle within reach instead of tucking it back in the fridge.

She'd never felt quite so ridiculous. Not even when wearing a bunny costume and reading badly rhymed poetry to a squirming herd of preschoolers.

There was no reason for the frantic fluttering of the butterflies in her stomach. It wasn't as if she was waiting for a knock on the door or even for the phone to ring. Yet she felt every bit as edgy as she had when waiting for Brad Wooten to pick her up for the junior prom. He had arrived right on time, posed for a few obligatory Polaroids, whisked her off to the prom in his Eddie Bauer Limited Edition Ford Explorer, then dumped her during the second verse of Green Day's "Good Riddance (Time of Your Life)" after his pep squad ex-girlfriend whispered in his ear that she wanted him back.

The two of them had celebrated their reunion by slipping away for a quickie in the backseat of that same Ford Explorer while Abby found a pay phone and called her dad to come and get her.

She'd managed to gulp back her tears until her father had pulled his battered Toyota into the back of the high school parking lot where they had agreed to meet, pushed open the car door from inside, and said, "Come on, baby. Let's go home."

She glanced at the digital clock in the corner of her computer screen. 6:56 p.m. A mere three seconds had ticked away since she'd last checked it. Considering how close she'd come to chickening out of their "date," it would be ironic if Mark was the one to stand her up. He'd probably found some voluptuous dark-eyed Italian beauty straight out of a Fellini film to help him crush some grapes between his toes and forgot all about her.

Catching a glimpse of her reflection in the screen only made Abby feel sillier. She'd actually traded her coffee-stained sweats for a black silk blouse and a pair of neatly creased linen slacks. She'd loosed her wavy mass of curls from their obligatory scrunchie, applied a touch of peach gloss to her lips, and dabbed a little Obsession behind each ear.

A fitting choice, considering she'd also shaved her legs and traded her comfy granny panties for a wisp of black lace a mere fraction of an inch away from being a thong.

Groaning, she dropped her head down on the

keyboard. If there was any hope of holding on to even a shred of her dwindling self-respect, she should do exactly what she knew Margo would do—close the laptop, take her de-scrunchied, perfumed, and nearly thonged self down to the nearest club, pick up the first passably good-looking stranger who asked her to dance, and bring him back to the apartment for some safe but anonymous sex.

Or close the laptop, walk to the freezer, dig out her emergency pint of Chunky Monkey, and wolf it down in one sitting while wistfully watching Colin Firth's Mr. Darcy emerge from the pond at Pemberley for the four-hundred-and-fifty-first time in the BBC version of *Pride and Prejudice*.

Either alternative beat sitting in front of the computer waiting to be picked up for a cyberdate by a man she knew so little about he was beginning to make the Phantom of the Opera seem like an extrovert.

She was reaching to close the laptop when a familiar chirp sent her pulse into overdrive.

Chapter Six

*M*arkBaynard: What are you wearing?

    Abby_Donovan: A spritz of Chanel No. 5 and the ice-blue satin evening gown Grace Kelly wore to accept her Oscar for THE COUNTRY GIRL. You?

MarkBaynard: Harrison Ford's leather bomber jacket from RAIDERS OF THE LOST ARK and Steve McQueen's Persol aviator glasses from THE GETAWAY.

Abby_Donovan: Speaking of getaways, I came this close to standing you up, you know.

MarkBaynard: Better offer?

Abby_Donovan: It's hard for any man to compete with Ben and Jerry.

MarkBaynard: I didn't know you were into threesomes.

Abby_Donovan: I was going to throw in Mr. Darcy and make it a foursome.

MarkBaynard: Naughty girl! And to think I had you pegged as a Brontë woman! How can you resist Heathcliff's smoldering good looks and incessant brooding?

Abby_Donovan: Heathcliff was a misogynistic asshole.

MarkBaynard: Could you explain that to my Lit 101 class? I hate to see all those impressionable young females swooning over him like he's Edward Cullen.

Abby_Donovan: I've always been Team Jacob myself. And Team Mr. Rochester.

MarkBaynard: So you don't mind if a guy keeps his mad wife locked up in the attic?

Abby_Donovan: Not if he puts the seat down after he uses the toilet. So where are we going tonight?

MarkBaynard: I found this charming little cafe in Volterra just a short walk from here. See what you think...

MarkBaynard: http://twitphoto.com/BM7stf

Abby_Donovan: Oh...it's darling! Hang on...let me grab my chiffon scarf and trade my heels for some sandals.

MarkBaynard: There's a cool breeze tonight. How about if I go all Cro-Magnon on you and drape my jacket over your shoulders?

Abby_Donovan: Mmm...thank you. It smells nice...like your aftershave. Is it Michel Germain?

MarkBaynard: Old Spice. I borrowed it from my grandfather.

Abby_Donovan: I wish you'd take off those shades. It makes me nervous when I can't see a man's eyes.

MarkBaynard: It would make you more nervous if you caught me staring at your chest while you talked instead of gazing deep into your eyes.

Abby_Donovan: Or if I caught you gazing deep into my eyes when I was hoping you were staring at my chest.

MarkBaynard: Ah, here we are. I reserved a candlelit table on the terrace. Would it offend your feminist sensibilities if I pulled your chair out for you?

Abby_Donovan: Not if you put the seat down after you use the toilet.

MarkBaynard: Do you like the music? I put in a special request.

Abby_Donovan: Very nice! What is it? Puccini's "O Mio Babbino Caro?"

MarkBaynard: No, Insane Clown Posse's "Somebody to Smoke Wit."

Abby_Donovan: OMGee...you are 15, aren't you?

MarkBaynard: What? Not a big hip-hop/thrash metal crossover fan?

Abby_Donovan: Not a big fan of insane clowns. Haven't you seen POLTERGEIST? Or read Stephen King's IT?

MarkBaynard: I prefer the more amiable charms of Ronald McDonald myself. It's the Hamburgler who creeps me out.

Abby_Donovan: I'm suddenly craving a Quarter Pounder. Maybe we should have just gone to McDonald's for dinner.

MarkBaynard: There's one right next to the KFC on the corner. Oops...too late! Here comes the waiter with the specials.

Abby_Donovan: So what are you having?

MarkBaynard: I'm in the mood for focaccia topped with fresh spinach and smoked gouda and the mascarpone ravioli in tomato vodka sauce. You?

Abby_Donovan: I believe I'll have the Chef Boyardee SpaghettiOs.

MarkBaynard: Let me ask the sommelier which vintage he recommends with those. Price, of course, is no object.

Abby_Donovan: Then I'll have the 1945 Mouton for $120,000.

MarkBaynard: You heard the lady. She'll have a Diet Coke.

Abby_Donovan: Cheapskate! I thought you'd pay for my wine with your trust fund.

MarkBaynard: Sorry. No trust fund until I turn 21, remember?

Abby_Donovan: Is this an awkward silence? Are you staring at my chest? I'm not sure what's supposed to happen next.

MarkBaynard: We get to know each other. Isn't that what people do on first dates?

Abby_Donovan: I've always heard you'll never have more in common than you do on your first date. Especially if you get married later.

MarkBaynard: I can vouch for that. As can my ex. So...toilet paper...over or under?

Abby_Donovan: I was a staunch "over" until I got up one night and Buffy had unrolled the entire roll with her paws. Ginger or Mary Ann?

MarkBaynard: Oh, definitely Mary Ann. Everybody knows those wholesome, corn-fed Kansas farm girls are easy.

Abby_Donovan: I'm betting you're a big Dorothy Gale fan.

MarkBaynard: I always preferred the Wicked Witch of the West myself. So passionate. So misunderstood. So green.

Abby_Donovan: What's not to love about a

woman willing to kill for a fabulous pair of shoes? Yankees or Red Sox?

MarkBaynard: Braves. I'm from Oxford, Mississippi, not Oxford, Connecticut. Gilligan or the Skipper?

Abby_Donovan: Thurston Howell III. Any man with that much money can call me "Lovey" and eat crackers in my bed all night long. Dorothy, Blanche, or Rose?

MarkBaynard: Sofia. Betty White will always be da bomb but I like a woman with experience. Angel or Spike?

Abby_Donovan: Spike. I never could resist a jerk with a Billy Idol complex, a Brit accent and a snarky sense of humor.

MarkBaynard: Whew! That's a relief. At least the jerk part.

Abby_Donovan: Best song of all time?

MarkBaynard: That's an easy one. The Who's "Baba O'Riley."

Abby_Donovan: Oh, I don't think so. That would be discounting the seminal influence on the pop/rock genre of David Cassidy's "I Think I Love You."

MarkBaynard: Do you?

Abby_Donovan: What?

MarkBaynard: Think you love me?

Abby_Donovan: Don't be impertinent. I'm not even sure I like you yet. Ah...here comes the food! The fresh tomatoes & rosemary smell incredible!

MarkBaynard: Shall we share a noodle like Lady and her Tramp?

Abby_Donovan: Not unless you want to get stabbed in the throat with a fork.

MarkBaynard: You're such an incurable romantic! (Dodging the serrated edge of yr bread knife, I reach over & gently tuck a strand of hair behind yr ear.)

MarkBaynard: Abby?

MarkBaynard: Abby? Did my charms sweep you off your feet or did a power surge knock you off the Internet?

Abby_Donovan: You caught me off guard. I think I might be blushing.

MarkBaynard: If you want me to keep my hands to myself, I will. I won't even lean over and lick the dab of marinara sauce from the corner of your mouth.

Abby_Donovan: Good. Because I don't believe in licking on the first date. Wait...did that sound as bad as I think it did?

MarkBaynard: Worse. Now I'm blushing.

Abby_Donovan: Perhaps we should just move on to the dessert course.

MarkBaynard: Cannoli, biscotti, or tiramasu?

Abby_Donovan: Mmm...cannoli.

MarkBaynard: The waiter wants to know if you'd like your cannoli dipped in chocolate.

Abby_Donovan: If I said that to you, it would sound really dirty.

MarkBaynard: Everything you say sounds dirty to me.

Abby Donovan: What I'd really like is a box of nice hot Krispy Kreme donuts.

MarkBaynard: Now you're just being a tease. Because I'd never be able to resist licking that glaze from the corner of your mouth.

Abby_Donovan: Or the bottom of the box.

MarkBaynard: Or the bottom of your shoe.

Abby_Donovan: Foot fetishist?

MarkBaynard: No...Krispy Kreme fetishist.

Abby_Donovan: Sigh...I may be falling in love with you after all.

MarkBaynard: If that's all it took, you just might be easier than Mary Ann. Or Ginger.

Abby_Donovan: Like everyone didn't know Ginger was diddling the Professor! That's why he never fixed the radio. He didn't want to get off that island.

MarkBaynard: If you could take one book on your 3-hour tour, what would it be?

Abby_Donovan: Peter S. Beagle's A FINE AND PRIVATE PLACE.

MarkBaynard: "The grave's a fine and private place. But none I think do there embrace." Andrew Marvell

Abby_Donovan: According to Mr. Beagle, Marvell was wrong.

MarkBaynard: How so?

Abby_Donovan: Because in the novel his characters learn to embrace both life and death and to realize it takes one to give the other meaning.

MarkBaynard: Is that what you believe? That life has more meaning because it's finite?

Abby_Donovan: I sense a note of skepticism.

MarkBaynard: I'm just not convinced the poor schlub who ends his life puking his guts out in a hospital trash can would agree with you.

Abby_Donovan: What about you? What do you believe?

MarkBaynard: That life has meaning simply because it's...life. You don't have to go out and wrap your BMW around a tree to find the value in it.

Abby_Donovan: Where does that leave death? Is it without meaning?

MarkBaynard: There are meaningful deaths. And there are absurd and utterly meaningless deaths. Unfortunately, you don't get to choose which one you get.

Abby_Donovan: Unless you're Sylvia Plath.

MarkBaynard: Is that why you have an electric oven? Less temptation?

Abby_Donovan: If I had my choice of overdramatic writer deaths, I'd prefer to walk into the water with my pockets full of rocks like Virginia Woolf. You?

MarkBaynard: Death of choice? Choking to death on a Krispy Kreme. Unless "none of the above" is an option.

Abby_Donovan: Only if you're a vampire. Which brings us back to Spike. Buffy or Faith?

MarkBaynard: Which brings us back to that threesome.

Abby_Donovan: Throw in Drusilla and you could make it a foursome.

MarkBaynard: I've always been more of a one-woman man myself. That's how I ended up marrying my high school sweetheart when I was only 22.

Abby_Donovan: You know, it just might be bad form to talk about your ex-wife on a first date.

MarkBaynard: Oh, I don't know. You never know when you might be interviewing your next ex-wife.

Abby_Donovan: How long were you married?

MarkBaynard: 9 years, 11 months and 17 days. Saved me from having to buy an expensive anniversary gift.

Abby_Donovan: Yeah, divorce lawyers are SO much cheaper. Were you the proverbial couple who got married too young?

MarkBaynard: Probably. By the time I was ready to grow up, she was ready to grow apart.

Abby_Donovan: Any kids?

MarkBaynard: A son. Dylan. He'll be four in November.

Abby_Donovan: I knew it! That's why you and Tinky Winky and Biff the Bunny are BFFs, isn't it?

MarkBaynard: Ah, Biff and his beloved hedgehog Henry/Henrietta. Their unrequited love is truly one for the ages. As long as the age is 3.

Abby_Donovan: Is your son named after Bob Dylan or Dylan Thomas?

MarkBaynard: Dylan from 90210. If we had twins I was going to name them Brandon and Brenda.

Abby_Donovan: Is he traveling with you?

MarkBaynard: No. He's with his mother at the moment. I hope to see him soon. So have you ever taken a stroll down the aisle?

Abby_Donovan: No. I was going steady for a while after I came to New York but he broke up with me before I could make him Mr. Abigail Donovan.

MarkBaynard: Threatened by your meteoric rise to fame?

Abby_Donovan: Turned out he preferred artists of the starving variety. Dumped me for a sculptor in Soho who had never even had a show.

MarkBaynard: What did she sculpt?

Abby_Donovan: Mostly plaster casts of his penis.

MarkBaynard: Specialized in miniatures, eh?

Abby_Donovan: Now I KNOW I'm falling in love with you.

MarkBaynard: Did he break your heart?

Abby_Donovan: In his defense, I'm not sure I ever really gave it to him. I prefer to keep it in my safe-deposit box at the bank.

MarkBaynard: Let me guess. You sleep with the key under your pillow.

Abby_Donovan: I'm beginning to think I might have lost it. Permanently.

MarkBaynard: I know this fabulous locksmith. I'll give you his number someday...

MarkBaynard: We're the last ones left in the cafe and I believe the hot-eyed Tuscan maître d' is giving us the evil eye. Shall we go?

Abby_Donovan: I'd say "Your place or mine?"

but since we've already established I don't lick on the first date...

MarkBaynard: It's still a lovely night. How about if I just walk you back to the villa where you're staying?

Abby_Donovan: The 16th-century villa with the marble floors, the frescoed ceiling painted by Michelangelo, and the climate-controlled wine cellar?

MarkBaynard: That would be the one. You are paying for dinner, right?

Abby_Donovan: So (I say as we stroll down a cobbled alleyway), how did you end up teaching English lit? A love of books or of shaping young minds?

MarkBaynard: A love of being tenured before I was thirty-five. The books and young minds were fringe benefits along with the 401(k) and the dental plan.

Abby_Donovan: I'm not buying your dime-store cynicism, Mr. Baynard. I'm convinced the wounded heart of a romantic beats beneath that sardonic exterior.

MarkBaynard: If you must know, I chose English lit because I wanted to wear one of those houndstooth jackets w/the leather patches on the elbows to work.

Abby_Donovan: It'll look fabulous on the dust jacket of your first novel.

MarkBaynard: Plus it was really the only possible vocational choice for a kid who used to carry a briefcase to grade school.

Abby_Donovan: I used to do that too!

MarkBaynard: Yeah, but if you're a girl they don't steal your lunch money and give you an atomic wedgie for it.

Abby_Donovan: You never did tell me what book an English lit professor would take on his 3-hour tour?

MarkBaynard: The Kama Sutra, of course. Especially if Ginger and Mary Ann were on board.

Abby_Donovan: And if you had to choose a book WITHOUT pictures? Tolstoy? Dickens? Updike?

MarkBaynard: No Biff the Bunny, huh? How about A PRAYER FOR OWEN MEANY by John Irving?

Abby_Donovan: Really? I would have pegged you as more of a Hunter S. Thompson man.

MarkBaynard: He was gonzo, but Irving, like Jerry Seinfeld, knows the only way to survive this life is to view it as some sort of absurdist tragicomedy.

Abby_Donovan: No matter how tragic or comic,

all of Irving's books incorporate a pervasive sense of destiny.

MarkBaynard: Maybe that's the secret appeal for me. In a John Irving novel, nobody ever dies a meaningless death. Ah, here we are back at your villa.

Abby_Donovan: Do you want your coat back?

MarkBaynard: Keep it. It'll give me an excuse to call you again.

Abby_Donovan: What makes you think I'll answer?

MarkBaynard: Because you care enough to play hard to get.

Abby_Donovan: Maybe I'm just bored because my hot Italian lover is off racing his Formula One Ferrari at Monza.

MarkBaynard: His loss. My gain.

Abby_Donovan: Why are you looking at me like that?

MarkBaynard: I'm trying to decide if I should kiss you goodnight.

Abby_Donovan: I'm trying to decide if I want you to kiss me.

MarkBaynard: I definitely want to kiss you but I don't want to scare you away.

Abby_Donovan: I don't frighten that easily.

MarkBaynard: Then why are you trembling? (I

lean down & ever so gently brush my lips against your temple, inhaling the scent of your strawberry shampoo.)

Abby_Donovan: It's Paul Mitchell. I haven't used strawberry shampoo since the 6th grade.

MarkBaynard: (Then I turn and walk away, the epitome of Steve McQueen cool, humming "Perfect Day" by Lou Reed while you gaze longingly after me.)

Abby_Donovan: Goodnight Sawyer (I call after you, admiring your carefully calculated slouch.)

MarkBaynard: Goodnight Freckles (I toss over my shoulder.)

Abby_Donovan: Goodnight Hurley

MarkBaynard: Goodnight Juliet

Abby_Donovan: Goodnight Dr. Jack

MarkBaynard: Goodnight Penny

Abby_Donovan: Goodnight Desmond

MarkBaynard: Goodnight Sun

Abby_Donovan: Goodnight Smoke Monster

MarkBaynard: Goodnight Tweetheart...

Long after Mark was gone, Abby continued to stare at her Tweetdeck through semidazed eyes. Several new tweets from people she was Following flitted across the left column of the screen, but her Direct Message column remained empty. It wasn't the screen she was seeing anyway, but a man walking away from her down a winding cobbled alleyway laced with moonlight and shadows.

He turned, glancing over his shoulder at her, his eyes filled with humor and tenderness. She frowned. No matter how hard she tried, she couldn't transpose anyone else's features over his. He wasn't Hugh Jackman or Jude Law or even Steve McQueen. He was just Mark. Her Mark.

Both friend and stranger.

She touched a hand to her cheek, remembering the odd tingle she had felt both times he had pretended to touch her. She tried to remember the last time she had felt that tingle—that unspoken promise that something magical was about to happen.

Had it been like that the first time Dean kissed her? She frowned, struggling to remember exactly where that kiss had taken place. Had it been on the steps of the Met after the Frida Kahlo exhibit? Or over the morel risotto at Balthazar on Spring Street? It had only been a little over a year since their breakup, but she could barely remember their first date, much less their first kiss. Even Dean's face was growing fuzzy in her memory, like some half-remembered actor from a black-and-white movie she'd seen as a child.

Surely she must have felt that tingle during

her freshman year at Wake Forest when she'd surrendered her body and her soul to a graphic arts student with killer abs, a pack-of-unfiltered-Camels-a-day cigarette habit, and the sleepy, dark-lashed eyes of a young Al Pacino. She had always been a good girl and he had been her first real bad-boy crush. Come to think of it, what she'd felt that night hadn't exactly been a tingle but more of a dizzying rush of lust, followed by a siren in her head warning her she was about to make a terrible mistake she would never regret.

Nope, she was pretty sure the last time she had felt that tingle was in the fourth grade when Chris McClain had passed her a note at lunch that said, "You're reall prety. If you give me your twinkie, I'll be your boyfriend." (Of course he had dumped her the following week for a girl whose mom packed Ho Hos in her New Kids on the Block lunchbox.)

So how to explain the delicious little thrill that had made the hair on the back of her neck stand up when Mark had simply pretended to brush his lips tenderly over her temple? Had Margo been right? Was he the perfect lover for a budding agoraphobic, a woman who had built so many walls around her heart she was in danger of ending up imprisoned behind them forever?

Abby absently reached for the glass of wine, grimacing when it touched her lips. Neglected and forgotten, the chardonnay in the bottom of the glass had grown warm while she sipped an imaginary Diet Coke with her imaginary date at a very real cafe on the other side of the world.

Chapter Seven

MarkBaynard: What are you wearing?

Abby_Donovan: Coffee-stained sweats & the Playboy Bunny ears and tail Elle Woods wore to the computer store in LEGALLY BLONDE. You?

MarkBaynard: The aluminum foil hat Joaquin Phoenix wore to ward off the alien mind control in SIGNS and Johnny Depp's "Wino Forever" tattoo.

Abby_Donovan: The tattoo that read "Winona" before he and Miss Ryder broke up?

MarkBaynard: That's the one. Just think—if I got your name tattooed on my ass, I could change it to "Flabby" after you dumped me.

Abby_Donovan: Be still, my heart! I was beginning to think you were one of those guys who don't tweet after a first date.

MarkBaynard: I didn't want to appear too eager...or too pathetic.

Abby_Donovan: Well, one out of two isn't bad.

MarkBaynard: Miss me?

Abby_Donovan: A little. I'm embarrassed to admit I caught myself tweeting to you in my head more than once over the past few days.

MarkBaynard: If I hadn't been wearing that aluminum foil hat, I might have heard you. What did you say?

Abby_Donovan: Just random observations: A day without cat hair in your coffee is like...a day without cat hair in your coffee.

Abby_Donovan: Don't they know that food really IS love?

Abby_Donovan: Do people who pee in the shower think they're multitasking?

MarkBaynard: Well, now that you mention it...

Abby_Donovan: Is there anyone who HASN'T made a sex tape with Pam Anderson?

MarkBaynard: Well, now that you mention it, there was that night in Rio...

Abby_Donovan: So where in the world is Mark Baynard today?

MarkBaynard: VIEW FROM MY iPHONE: http://twitphoto.com/MB7stg

Abby_Donovan: You finally made it to Florence, Alabama! Tell me what you're doing so I can live vicariously through you.

MarkBaynard: Sitting in front of the Neptune Fountain at the Piazza della Signoria, listening to the bells of San Miniato chime the hour.

Abby_Donovan: Sigh...I'm sitting in front of a cold bowl of oatmeal, listening to Buffy the Mouse Slayer cough up a hair ball on my carpet.

MarkBaynard: So how is the writing going today?

Abby_Donovan: VIEW FROM MY LAPTOP: http://tweetpic.com/2825190611

MarkBaynard: Should I ask why you have a stuffed gorilla climbing over the back of your computer? Or why you have a stuffed gorilla?

Abby_Donovan: I'm hoping he'll carry me away to the top of the Empire State Building if I don't agree to become his bride.

MarkBaynard: Another bad writing day?

Abby_Donovan: It's shaping up to be a 2 frappucino day. One for a.m. of boundless optimism. One for p.m. of utter despair.

MarkBaynard: Have you thought about supplementing your writing income with an endorsement deal from Starbucks?

Abby_Donovan: Edgar Allan Poe had his opium and I have my frappucinos. Such is the plight of the tortured artist.

MarkBaynard: At least if you end up in the gutter like Poe, sympathetic gawkers can toss quarters into your little plastic cup.

Abby_Donovan: Which I'll probably use to buy more frappucinos.

MarkBaynard: Maybe a second trip to Starbucks wouldn't be a bad idea. You might need a change of scenery.

Abby_Donovan: This morning I saw one of the cats out of the corner of my eye & started talking to it. Then I realized it was my house shoe.

MarkBaynard: It's worse if you don't have a cat. And you just drank a pitcher of bellinis. So what have you written today?

Abby_Donovan: Seven Facebook updates, a guest blog, and about 400 tweets.

MarkBaynard: So roughly the equivalent of a long novella, right?

Abby_Donovan: Yep. Except I didn't get paid for any of it.

MarkBaynard: No one will respect you if you're giving it away for free.

Abby_Donovan: That's what Mama told me when I was in high school. I just don't understand why I can't get paid for tweeting.

MarkBaynard: I could send you a dime for each Direct Message.

Abby_Donovan: Make it a dollar and you've got a deal.

MarkBaynard: You must be doing something right. I noticed you're up to 666 Followers.

Abby_Donovan: Should I be alarmed?

MarkBaynard: Only if you start to hear the theme from THE OMEN in your head.

Abby_Donovan: Do you think obsessive tweeting counts as a hobby or an addiction?

MarkBaynard: A hobby. That's what I used to tell myself about THE LEGEND OF ZELDA after I'd been playing for 37 hours without food or sleep.

Abby_Donovan: Sometimes I think I can't write because the Internet is smothering my brain with minutiae. Did you know it was Cankle Awareness Month?

MarkBaynard: What in the hell is a cankle? Is it contagious? Sexually transmitted?

Abby_Donovan: It's what happens when your ankle disappears beneath a layer of fat and your calf looks like it's attached directly to your foot.

MarkBaynard: I'm so glad to see attention being brought to such a dreaded medical condition. Is there a foundation I can donate to?

Abby_Donovan: You wouldn't be laughing if YOU had them.

MarkBaynard: Oddly enough, I think I would. So what prompted you to become a writer in the first place?

Abby_Donovan: I felt like I had something to say about my life. A story to tell. But now that I've told that story...

MarkBaynard: Maybe it's time for you to tell someone else's story.

Abby_Donovan: Aren't you supposed to write what you know?

MarkBaynard: I always thought it would be more fun to write what I didn't know. I figured that would give me a lifetime of material.

Abby_Donovan: I haven't told a soul this, but sometimes I think I'd have been better off if my first book hadn't shot to the top of the bestseller list.

MarkBaynard: Ah...the romantic fantasy of toiling in obscurity! You could be starving in a garret instead of a posh apartment overlooking Central Park.

Abby_Donovan: How did you know I lived in a posh apartment?

MarkBaynard: Because it overlooks Central Park.

Abby_Donovan: When you start out at the top, where else is there to go but down?

MarkBaynard: Maybe it's more like a roller

coaster—a downward swoop followed by a slow &
steady climb to the highest peak of all.

Abby_Donovan: Roller coasters make me hurl.

MarkBaynard: Then maybe it's more like a Tilt-
A-Whirl. Oh, wait...Tilt-A-Whirls make me hurl.

Abby_Donovan: So when are you going to start
writing YOUR novel? (she asked pointedly)

MarkBaynard: I'm (cough, cough) still in the
planning stages. Well, actually I'm just planning to
plan. Haven't made it as far as planning to write yet.

Abby_Donovan: Sigh...I remember those days.
I always "nest" before diving into a project. Dust
the baseboards. Put all my photos in albums, etc.

MarkBaynard: I think that's called stalling.

Abby_Donovan: I prefer procrastination, thank
you very much.

MarkBaynard: Maybe you just need to learn
to embrace your natural rhythms—in life and in
writing.

Abby_Donovan: Even if my natural rhythm
seems to be complete indolence followed by hys-
terical bursts of panicked activity?

MarkBaynard: Works for me. Although I
haven't actually made it to the panicked stage yet.
Or the activity.

Abby_Donovan: What are you interested in
writing about?

MarkBaynard: A witty, talented woman who meets a mysterious but strangely irresistible man on Twitter.

Abby_Donovan: Who then comes to her posh apartment off of Central Park in the middle of the night and murders her with an ax?

MarkBaynard: Have chloroform, will travel. Would you mind leaving a key under the mat? Not so good at breaking & entering.

Abby_Donovan: No mat, but I'll be sure to leave your name with my doorman and tell maintenance to stock up on bleach and Hefty bags.

MarkBaynard: Don't forget the lye and the 50-gallon drum.

Abby_Donovan: My friend Margo tried to warn me about you. Said you were probably really an escaped convict.

MarkBaynard: Don't be ridiculous. They'd have to catch me first.

Abby_Donovan: When I told her about our "tweet date," she told me about something called…(dare I speak its name aloud?)…tweetsex?

MarkBaynard: I think I just saw two sparrows having that outside the window of my bed-and-breakfast. Looked like fun.

Abby_Donovan: Sex in 140 characters or less. Have you ever heard of anything so ridiculous?

MarkBaynard: That depends. Are there also tweetgasms?

Abby_Donovan: I think it sounds completely dehumanizing.

MarkBaynard: I'm a guy. We never turn down sex, no matter how ridiculous. Or dehuman. I think we should try it. You go first.

Abby_Donovan: You've GOT to be kidding me.

MarkBaynard: I haven't decided yet. Try it and I'll let you know.

Abby_Donovan: You're laughing at me, aren't you? I'M not wearing an aluminum foil hat. I can hear you!

MarkBaynard: What do you have to lose?

Abby_Donovan: Besides my pride? My dignity? My self-respect?

MarkBaynard: Coward! Chicken! Cluck...cluck... cluck...

Abby_Donovan: If you think I'm going to let you peer pressure me into doing something so inane, so ridiculous, so unspeakably demeaning...

MarkBaynard: I triple dog dare you.

Abby_Donovan:...then you can just close your eyes and imagine me slowly running my hot, wet tongue along the throbbing length of your...

MarkBaynard: Um, Abby...you sort of forgot to

make that last tweet a Direct Message. Which means all 666 of your Followers just read it.

Abby_Donovan: Oh God.

MarkBaynard: And all your male Followers just closed their eyes to imagine you slowly running your hot, wet tongue along the throbbing lengths of their...

Abby_Donovan: Oh. My. God.

MarkBaynard: But look! You're up to 678 Followers now!

MarkBaynard: 682!

MarkBaynard: 706!

MarkBaynard: 732! Man, you are hotter than Br*tney Freaking Sp*ars!

Abby_Donovan: I wish I was dead.

MarkBaynard: Are you blushing? You're so adorable when you blush.

Abby_Donovan: I wish YOU were dead.

MarkBaynard: I was only joking with you! I didn't think you'd really do it. 747!

Abby_Donovan: I will hunt you down. It may take me the rest of my life, but I WILL find you. And when I do, you will suffer a slow, excruciating death.

MarkBaynard: It'll take more than that to scare me. I've already survived 3 hours of sitting through the stage production of THE LION KING.

Abby_Donovan: I have to go now. Maybe it's not too late to sign up for the Witness Protection Program.

MarkBaynard: 756!

Abby_Donovan: Goodnight Cousin Itt (she said with withering scorn)

MarkBaynard: Goodnight Cara Mia (he replied tenderly in a faux Italian accent)

Abby_Donovan: Goodnight Thing

MarkBaynard: Goodnight Wednesday

Abby_Donovan: Goodnight Pugsley

MarkBaynard: Goodnight Grandma

Abby_Donovan: Goodnight Lurch

MarkBaynard: Goodnight Tweetheart...

Saturday, May 21—3:37 P.M.

MarkBaynard: What are you wearing?

Abby_Donovan: Coffee-stained sweats and Audrey Hepburn's tiara from BREAKFAST AT TIFFANY'S. You?

MarkBaynard: Tim Allen's uniform with the torn sleeve from GALAXY QUEST and Igor's hump from YOUNG FRANKENSTEIN.

Abby_Donovan: What hump?

MarkBaynard: Now it's my turn to propose.

Will you come live w/me and be my love & watch YOUNG FRANKENSTEIN &/or BLAZING SADDLES at least once a week?

Abby_Donovan: Throw in CADDYSHACK, ANIMAL HOUSE & AIRPLANE and you've got a deal.

MarkBaynard: Will you have my babies too?

Abby_Donovan: Stop trying to sweet-talk me. I'm still sulking.

MarkBaynard: Why? Thanks to me, you're up to 1075 Followers!

Abby_Donovan: Followers...stalkers...predators...it's all semantics.

MarkBaynard: Only when it comes to getting the restraining orders.

Abby_Donovan: Do you know how many people I've had to Block in the past two days?

MarkBaynard: 452?

Abby_Donovan: I've gotten dozens of dirty tweets, 4 marriage proposals & an exorcism chant from a voodoo priest who wants to drive out my sexual demons.

MarkBaynard: So which offer are you going to accept?

Abby_Donovan: Probably the one from the hit man offering to trade his skills for my sexual favors. So where will you be next week?

MarkBaynard: At the bottom of the Hudson River, if you and your new boyfriend have anything to say about it.

Abby_Donovan: If I wasn't in such an expansive mood, I wouldn't be tweeting to you at all.

MarkBaynard: I thought I sensed a disturbance in the force. Why so non-serious?

Abby_Donovan: VIEW FROM MY LAPTOP: http://tweetpic.com/2825190612

MarkBaynard: Is that Donkey from SHREK? He looks a lot happier than the gorilla.

Abby_Donovan: That's because something wonderful finally happened to me today.

MarkBaynard: You started Chapter Six?

Abby_Donovan: Not quite THAT wonderful, although I did get some intriguing new ideas after we tweeted the other day.

MarkBaynard: That's me. Mark Baynard, English lit professor and inspiration to women everywhere.

Abby_Donovan: I'm excited because my agent called to tell me my editor wants to have lunch with us at Le Bernardin on Monday.

MarkBaynard: Are you excited about seeing your editor or getting a free lunch at some swanky French joint?

Abby_Donovan: Both, actually. My editor hasn't

been very receptive to my phone calls lately so I'm going to assume this is a Very Good Sign.

MarkBaynard: Like Sandra-Bullock-Starring-In-The-Movie-Of-Your-Book Very Good Sign?

Abby_Donovan: I like Sandra, but I was kind of hoping for Kate Winslet or Renée Zellweger.

MarkBaynard: I heard Pam Anderson was available.

Abby_Donovan: It wouldn't be THAT kind of movie.

MarkBaynard: It would if Pam Anderson was in it.

Abby_Donovan: Once I show my editor the first five chapters & share my new ideas, I'm hoping she won't mind granting me another deadline extension.

MarkBaynard: Just how many extensions has she granted you so far?

Abby_Donovan: I can't hear you! I think you're breaking up! Are you going through a tunnel?

MarkBaynard: That many, eh?

Abby_Donovan: I just haven't been able to make that much progress since I lost my dad. Maybe I just need to feel like somebody still believes in me.

MarkBaynard: I believe in you. But I don't think that's going to matter a whole hell of a lot until you start believing in yourself.

Abby_Donovan: Thank you very much, Dr. Phil.

MarkBaynard: I like to think of myself as more of a butch Deanna Troi. Or maybe Yoda during his Dagobah swamp phase.

Abby_Donovan: Just what every writer needs. The Jedi master of misplaced pronouns.

MarkBaynard: Deeply offended am I by your heartless mockery.

Abby_Donovan: Pretentious little muppet! And while we're on the subject, you look just like Miss Piggy when you try to do kung fu.

MarkBaynard: You're still talking to Yoda, right? Because I look a lot more like the Swedish Chef when I try to do kung fu.

Abby_Donovan: The Swedish Chef could probably kick Yoda's butt. Especially with those cleavers.

MarkBaynard: Should I be supportive by asking you what you're going to wear to your lunch?

Abby_Donovan: Not unless you're Adam Lambert. Do you really care what I'm going to wear?

MarkBaynard: No.

Abby_Donovan: Me neither. I'm the only woman I know who hates shopping for clothes. I wish elves would come to my apartment every morning & dress me.

MarkBaynard: Yeah, but then you'd end up with those pointy shoes with the bells on them.

Abby_Donovan: At least the birds could hear me coming.

MarkBaynard: You should do what Einstein did. Have an identical suit for every day of the week. Conserved his brain power for more important activities.

Abby_Donovan: Like coming up with the Theory of Relativity and exploring the mind of God? Or tweeting?

MarkBaynard: I heard Einstein was more of a Facebook fan. I think he invented Mafia Wars, didn't he?

Abby_Donovan: I believe it was Farmville. Or maybe Relativityville.

MarkBaynard: It's all relative, isn't it? What if WE had met on Facebook?

Abby_Donovan: We'd probably be married by now.

MarkBaynard: And have two kids.

Abby_Donovan: And a hybrid SUV.

MarkBaynard: And a second mortgage.

Abby_Donovan: And a vacation home in the Hamptons.

MarkBaynard: And...oh, the hell with it. If we

had met on Facebook, we'd have been divorced by now.

Abby_Donovan: Probably because you wouldn't help me pick out the right shoes for this meeting with my editor.

MarkBaynard: Forget the shoes. What you need is the right attitude.

Abby_Donovan: Uh-oh. Now I'm REALLY in trouble.

MarkBaynard: Try picturing yourself at this lunch looking productive and confident and successful beyond your wildest dreams.

Abby_Donovan: Add "blissfully naive" and "Oprah Winfrey" to the lunch and you'll be describing the person I was four years ago.

MarkBaynard: I probably wouldn't have liked her nearly as much as I like you. Bitter, jaded women are so much more fun.

Abby_Donovan: Maybe I should picture myself as Bette Davis in ALL ABOUT EVE. I'll go out and buy a cigarette holder this afternoon.

MarkBaynard: Or better yet, Sharon Stone in BASIC INSTINCT. But with underwear. Or not.

Abby_Donovan: My massage therapist (when I could still afford one) was a big believer in guided visualization...

Abby_Donovan: "You're walking through the shady woods when you see a chattering squirrel."

MarkBaynard: What if it's rabid?

Abby_Donovan: I'd rather be "lying on a sun-drenched balcony when Russell Crowe wanders over wearing only his loincloth from GLADIATOR."

MarkBaynard: Funny, but I never think about Russell during a massage.

Abby_Donovan: I had you pegged as more of a Clooney man.

MarkBaynard: If you want to know the truth, I've never had a massage.

Abby_Donovan: Oh, you poor deprived creature! I just love to pay strangers money to rub my body!

MarkBaynard: Good thing that was a Direct Message or you would have gained another 342 Followers/Stalkers/Predators.

Abby_Donovan: My massage therapist was a woman, which made it a little awkward when I blurted out "Will you marry me?" while she was rubbing my earlobes.

MarkBaynard: Not if you're getting a massage in the Meatpacking District.

Abby_Donovan: Have you spent much time in

New York or are you just one of those closeted straight male fans of SEX AND THE CITY?

MarkBaynard: I taught high school English for 5 years while I was getting my master's. I used to take my seniors to NYC every spring for a Broadway play.

Abby_Donovan: I came for a long weekend to visit my agent four years ago, fell in love with the city & never left.

MarkBaynard: Did your parents put your picture on a milk carton?

Abby_Donovan: The hardest part about leaving North Carolina was leaving them, especially since my mom had just gone into the nursing home...

Abby_Donovan: But Daddy wanted me to follow my dreams. He told me that's what my mom would want too...if she hadn't thought it was still 1992 and I was 10.

MarkBaynard: I spent most of my time in New York making sure my students didn't get mugged or pregnant.

Abby_Donovan: I bet you were one of those uber-cool teachers like Mr. Chips, weren't you?

MarkBaynard: I was more like Mr. Kotter or that guy from GLEE who looks like the love child of Orlando Bloom & Justin Timberlake.

Abby_Donovan: Your female students were probably writing "I love you" on their eyelids and listening to "Don't Stand So Close to Me" on their Walkmans.

MarkBaynard: Occupational hazard for any young male teacher w/an earnest appreciation for CATCHER IN THE RYE & hair he can't afford to keep trimmed.

Abby_Donovan: Did your wife mind all of that nubile female adoration?

MarkBaynard: I don't think she even noticed. Look, I'm going to be unplugged for a few days. But I promise to check in as soon as I get back.

Abby_Donovan: Cheating on me with another Follower, eh? Does she give better tweetsex than I do?

MarkBaynard: Baby, nobody does it better than you. Especially not when you wrap your hot, wet tongue around my throbbing...

Abby_Donovan: Mark Baynard, don't you dare!

MarkBaynard: Oops...sorry...I digress...Break a leg at the lunch, dollface. Or at least an elbow.

Abby_Donovan: Goodnight Mr. Schuester

MarkBaynard: Goodnight Miss Pillsbury

Abby_Donovan: Goodnight Puck

MarkBaynard: Goodnight Rachel

Abby_Donovan: Goodnight Kurt

MarkBaynard: Goodnight Quinn

Abby_Donovan: Goodnight Finn

MarkBaynard: Goodnight Sue Sylvester, you heartless but oddly sexy beast

Abby_Donovan: Goodnight Artie

MarkBaynard: Goodnight Tweetheart...

Chapter Eight

*L*e Bernardin was located on West Fifty-first Street, in the very heart of the Theater District. Its ivory linen tablecloths and sleek teak accents created the perfect marriage between mellow old-world elegance and modern design. Dark oil paintings adorned the light walls. Graceful sprays of fresh cherry blossoms bloomed from tall glass vases perched on marble-topped dividers, giving many of the tables a carefully crafted illusion of privacy. The tasteful strains of Ravel's *Pavane* drifting from the invisible loudspeakers wove a melodic counterpoint through the hushed murmur of conversation and the muffled clink of silverware against expensive china. The restaurant smelled of the genuine leather padding of its chairs, fresh fish swimming in a succulent sea of *beurre blanc*, and money, both old and new.

It was a place where the stars of stage, screen, and Wall Street came to eat in four-star elegance.

A place where careers were launched, fortunes were made, and hearts were won.

Just stepping through the glass doors of the restaurant and breathing the rarified air made Abby feel a little light-headed. A smiling hostess with a sleek blond bob took her name and went to see if the rest of her party had arrived. Abby clutched the leather portfolio containing the first five chapters of her book, plus the new notes she had scribbled down after her last tweet session with Mark, and peered discreetly around the restaurant, trying to look as if she still belonged there. Her recent culinary experiences had been limited to ordering Chinese takeout from Hop Lo's or soup from Hale and Hearty. It seemed as if a lifetime had passed since she'd been wined and dined on a nightly basis at trendy eateries like Craft, Masa, and Momofuku. She bit back a smile, wondering what Mark would have to say about *that* name.

She'd taken his advice and armored herself in her favorite dress-to-kick-ass ensemble. She'd actually worn the form-fitting black pencil skirt and coral double-breasted Ralph Lauren jacket on Oprah's show at the peak of her success. Since she'd spent more hours in the consoling arms of Ben and Jerry than at the gym recently, it had taken an industrial-strength pair of Spanx to squeeze her into the skirt. She was afraid it might take the Jaws of Life to get her out of it.

The hostess returned to escort her to the table. Her agent and editor were already deep in conversation. Her editor was a statuesque brunette with impeccable taste in both fashion and literature and the creamy Botoxed brow and cherry red lips of an aging Snow White. Her agent was a petite and unassuming-looking blonde who swore like a cast member of *Jersey Shore* and fought like a Valkyrie for her clients.

Both women abruptly stopped talking and rose from their chairs as Abby made her way toward the table, their welcoming smiles a shade too bright.

Abby felt her own smile begin to falter. By the time greetings were murmured and air kisses traded all around, she knew exactly how Jesus must have felt when Judas asked him to pass the bread basket at the Last Supper. She could almost smell the notes of guilt and regret beneath the delicate jasmine fragrance of the Jean Patou perfume her editor always wore.

While the sommelier went to fetch their wine selection and Abby gazed blindly at the menu, they dispensed with the obligatory small talk. They asked about her mother. She asked them about their husbands and children. Nobody asked about the leather portfolio she had discreetly tucked beneath the table. Ravel faded, making way for the mournful notes of a Bach cello solo. Abby polished off an exquisite appetizer of sautéed calamari filled with sweet prawns and shiitake mushrooms without tasting a bite.

Their entrées and the moment of reckoning arrived with a tasteful flourish of violins thoughtfully provided by Vivaldi. While her agent sat in mute misery, nursing a beautifully plated portion of pan-roasted monkfish, her editor set aside her fork and began to speak. Her words came to Abby's ears in staccato sound bytes filtered through a nearly intolerable tone of kindness.

" . . . difficult economy . . . "

" . . . decreased leisure spending . . . "

" . . . altering book market . . . "

" . . . corporate cuts . . . "

" . . . in-house layoffs . . . "

" . . . so sorry . . . "

" . . . wish things were different . . . "

" . . . still believe in you . . . "

" . . . thoroughly confident an author with your talent will land on her feet . . . "

As her editor continued to dissect the publishing economy and crush the last of her dreams, Abby was forced to nod in sympathetic understanding while her warm lobster carpaccio turned to sawdust in her mouth. Before the waiter could return with the dessert menu, her editor's Black-Berry and her agent's iPhone chimed almost simultaneously.

"Damn," her editor said, making a valiant effort to overcome the Botox long enough to scowl at the text message drifting across the screen of her Black-Berry. "I'm afraid I'm going to have to duck out early. The art department is having a cover crisis over Lindsay Lohan's new autobiography. They can't decide if she should wear Versace or an orange jumpsuit."

"And that was my dentist's office." Her agent tucked her iPhone back into her Coach bag as she rose. "I completely forgot about the root canal I had scheduled for this afternoon!"

After another awkward round of air kisses, during which Abby's agent murmured in her ear, "I'll call you tonight," they departed like hostages fleeing the scene of a bank robbery, leaving Abby sitting all alone at the table.

She slowly pushed her plate away, not sure whether she should be mourning the fact that her career was over or that she'd just wasted an exquisitely delicious hundred-dollar entrée. Since Le Bernardin was as well known for its flawless

French service as it was for its culinary charms, the waiter came rushing over the instant her fingertips left the plate.

If he pitied her for being abandoned so abruptly by her lunch companions, he hid it behind a veneer of impeccable courtesy. "The woman in black took care of the check," he informed her, referring to her editor. Her *former* editor. "She said you should help yourself to anything else you liked. Would you care to see the dessert menu?"

"No, thank you," Abby murmured. Not even the restaurant's legendary Chocolate-Chicory with dark chocolate cremeux and chicory ice cream could tempt her at the moment. Her stomach was still churning with disbelief.

The waiter continued to hover over her, but when she showed no sign of rising and surrendering her table to the next patron, he smiled awkwardly. "Just let me know if I can get you anything else."

As he started to turn away, Abby felt herself being swallowed by a bubble of panic. This was the last time her publisher would ever pick up the tab for her. It wouldn't be long before they found another golden girl to wine and dine, that is, if they hadn't already done so.

"Just a minute, please!" Abby didn't realize

she'd spoken so loudly until several of the diners at the surrounding tables interrupted their conversations and swiveled around to stare at her. "I believe I'd like some wine."

"Very good, ma'am." The waiter smiled with genuine pleasure at the prospect of being needed again. "I'll be right back with the wine list."

"That won't be necessary," Abby said, stopping him in his tracks. She smiled up at him, having already chosen the perfect vintage to celebrate a not-so-special occasion. "I'll have a bottle of Dom Pérignon. To go."

"I really thought I'd have another good year or two before I was reduced to swilling wine out of a paper sack in Central Park," Abby said matter-of-factly, passing the sack—and the bottle—to Margo.

"At least it's not cheap wine," Margo replied, tilting the bottle of vintage champagne to her lips for a long swig. She was courteous enough to wipe the bright scarlet lipstick stain off the bottle's mouth before handing it back to Abby.

"Cheers," Abby muttered before taking another drink. She was forced to pinch back a sneeze as the crisp bubbles burned her nose.

She and Margo were sitting on one of the long wooden benches that flanked the Poet's Walk. The late-spring sunshine drifted through the branches of the towering oaks that lined the walk, dappling their faces. Her friend had answered her distress signal without delay, although Abby couldn't have said whether it was the quaver in Abby's voice or the promise of Dom Pérignon that had lured Margo away from her weekly pedicure.

Margo wrested the bottle from Abby's hand and hefted it in a toast, sloshing champagne down the front of her lavender silk cardigan. "Here's to all the bastards who ever let us down! Screw 'em! Screw 'em all, I say! At least the ones we didn't already screw."

Margo could toss back tequila shots like a grizzled California biker, but she had always been a lightweight when it came to wine. A few more swallows and she'd be singing Lady Gaga and demonstrating cheer routines from her high school pep squad for anyone she could get to stop and watch her.

Abby gently plucked the bottle from her friend's hand, setting it on the ground next to her feet before Margo could notice. "That's the worst part of all this. I don't even have the satisfaction of being angry at them for dumping me. They didn't let me down. I let them down."

Draping an arm around Abby's shoulder, Margo gave her a bone-crunching squeeze. "You've never let me down."

"You've never paid me a lot of money to write a book I didn't finish."

"But you were going to finish it, weren't you?" Margo nudged the leather portfolio resting against the leg of the park bench with the gleaming patent leather toe of her pump. "You've got the proof right there."

"Do I?" Abby asked. "Or was I just using that to con myself into thinking I could do it? To make myself believe lightning really could strike twice in the same place?"

Margo sighed and rested her head on Abby's shoulder, no easy feat since she towered over Abby by at least half a foot. "I don't give a damn if you're not a bestselling author. You'll still be my best friend."

Abby rested her cheek against Margo's head. "And I don't give a damn if you're drunk off your ass. You'll still be mine."

Margo sat up abruptly, her eyes widening as she smothered a burp behind her cupped hand. "I don't feel so good all of a sudden."

"C'mon," Abby said, rising and tugging her

friend to her unsteady feet. "I'd better get you up to my apartment before you puke all over your Prada pumps."

"Do you have any tequila?" Margo asked hopefully as Abby left her swaying on the walk just long enough to retrieve her portfolio and sling it carelessly over one shoulder.

"No. But I have something even better. Coffee and ice cream."

They'd barely taken three steps before a man with a long, dirty beard and a faded army jacket staggered out from behind a tree to claim what was left of the bottle of Dom Pérignon.

Chapter Nine

Monday, May 30—9:24 P.M.

MarkBaynard: What are you wearing?

Abby_Donovan: Coffee-stained sweat-pants and Phoebe Cates's red bikini top from FAST TIMES AT RIDGEMONT HIGH.

MarkBaynard: If you'll excuse me, I think I need a moment of privacy in the bathroom.

Abby_Donovan: So what are you wearing?

MarkBaynard: Burt Reynolds's hat from SMOKEY AND THE BANDIT and John Cusack's black coat and tie from GROSSE POINT BLANK.

Abby_Donovan: Good. Maybe you could use a fork to kill me like he killed the president of Paraguay.

MarkBaynard: Would this be a bad time to ask how your lunch went?

Abby_Donovan: Let me put it this way—like you, I am now on sabbatical. Only in my business, we call it "fired."

MarkBaynard: Your publisher FIRED you? Can they do that?

Abby_Donovan: They can if you're late on your deadline and they threaten to declare you in breach of contract.

MarkBaynard: So maybe you should start with the appetizers.

Abby_Donovan: It all began with the murmur of discreet conversation followed by the sound of my heart breaking.

MarkBaynard: When did you realize something was wrong?

Abby_Donovan: The minute I saw my agent and editor. Their air kisses were too tragically tender.

MarkBaynard: Was there tongue involved? Because that's never a good sign with an air kiss.

Abby_Donovan: No tongue. Although I did get the sinking feeling I was about to get screwed.

MarkBaynard: At least they bought you lunch first, right?

Abby_Donovan: It was like one of those breakups on TV where the guy takes the girl to a ritzy restaurant so she can't make a scene when he dumps her.

MarkBaynard: Did you make a scene?

Abby_Donovan: Of course not. I was a complete adult about the whole thing.

MarkBaynard: So you ordered the most expensive thing on the menu, right?

Abby_Donovan: I used tremendous restraint. Well, except for the Dom Perignon.

MarkBaynard: Ah, the literary equivalent of emptying the mini-bar on your final business trip after your company forces you into early retirement!

Abby_Donovan: I would have stolen the napkins and ordered porn but they didn't have BOOTY AND THE BEAST or BARELY LEGALLY BLONDE on the menu.

MarkBaynard: Why did they let you go?

Abby_Donovan: Tough economy...blah blah blah...flagging sales throughout the industry...yadda yadda yadda...

MarkBaynard: I hate it when they tell you the truth.

Abby_Donovan: My poor editor is even fighting for HER job. My advance was fairly substantial so this will allow her to put some black back into her books.

MarkBaynard: They want their money back???

Abby_Donovan: Which wouldn't be a problem if I hadn't already spent it on shameless luxuries...like food...electricity...kibble for the cats...frappucinos.

MarkBaynard: What are you going to do?

Abby_Donovan: I'm considering suicide by paper cut.

MarkBaynard: Step away from the Chinese takeout menus. How did your agent react?

Abby_Donovan: She called later and made soothing noises about selling the book to another publisher. Which would be a fine strategy...if there was a book.

MarkBaynard: At least SHE didn't dump you.

Abby_Donovan: I wouldn't have blamed her if she had. I knew it was only a matter of time before the whole world discovered I was a talentless fraud.

MarkBaynard: A fraud whose very first novel made your publisher and agent a slew of cash and almost won the Pulitzer Prize for literature?

Abby_Donovan: "Almost" being the operative word.

MarkBaynard: Abby, the problem isn't that you can't write. It's that you're NOT writing.

Abby_Donovan: Et tu, Brute?

MarkBaynard: If your agent had a completed manuscript in her hot little hands, what are the odds she could sell it?

Abby_Donovan: Pretty high, I guess. It usually takes New York at least 5 books to figure out you're a pathetic washed-up has-been.

MarkBaynard: If she sold it, you could pay back your advance to the first publisher and still have enough left over to buy a little kibble, right?

Abby_Donovan: And maybe a frappucino or two.

MarkBaynard: Then take those rocks out of your pockets, call your agent & tell her you'll have a finished book on her desk by the end of the summer.

Abby_Donovan: Hasn't anyone ever told you that women just want men to LISTEN to them, not try to solve their problems for them?

MarkBaynard: My wife tried but I was too busy solving her problems to listen.

Abby_Donovan: I don't even know if I can have a finished book by the end of next year, much less this one.

MarkBaynard: You'll never find out if you don't sit your ass down in the chair and try.

Abby_Donovan: I thought you were supposed to be a DEmotivational speaker? You are SO fired. Sniff...sniff...

MarkBaynard: Oh God, you're not crying, are you? I feel so helpless when women cry. What in the hell am I supposed to do?

Abby_Donovan: You could pat me on the back and murmur, "Poor dear...poor, poor dear" in a soothing tone. Or make me some hot tea.

MarkBaynard: Who do I look like? Julie Freaking Andrews? Screw that. I'm going to the fridge and getting you a nice cold beer.

Abby_Donovan: While you're there, could you bring me the pint of Chunky Monkey? And a spoon?

MarkBaynard: Drink your beer float & listen to me. When you wrote yr 1st book, did U ever dream it was going to be welcomed by the world w/open arms?

Abby_Donovan: I didn't write it for the whole world. I wrote it for me.

MarkBaynard: Then that's what you need to do again. Write yourself another book.

Abby_Donovan: But I know in my heart I'll never write anything as good as that book.

MarkBaynard: Then write a piece of crap. It doesn't matter what you write as long as you stop beating yourself up about not writing and start writing.

Abby_Donovan: I don't love you anymore. I don't even like you. And I won't marry you, not even if you do know the name of Veronica Mars's dog.

MarkBaynard: Does this mean no more tweetsex?

Abby_Donovan: I'll be too tired for tweetsex.

I'll be too busy writing this stupid book. So you can just wrap your own tongue around your throbbing...

MarkBaynard: That's my girl. Now go call your agent. Tell her you've had a breakthrough.

Abby_Donovan: A breakthrough or a breakdown?

MarkBaynard: Whatever gets you to Chapter Six.

Abby_Donovan: I'm afraid, Mark. What if I can't do it?

MarkBaynard: We're all afraid, Abby.

Abby_Donovan: Oh, yeah. What are you afraid of?

MarkBaynard: The same things you are. Taking the wrong chance. Not being there for the people who depend on you.

Abby_Donovan: Is that all you've got? No homespun homilies? No motivational mantras? Where did Yoda go when I need him?

MarkBaynard: Back to that swamp in Dagobah to practice his kung fu.

Abby_Donovan: Shifty little muppet.

MarkBaynard: The force may not be with you, Abby. But I will be.

Abby_Donovan: Goodnight House

MarkBaynard: Goodnight Cuddy

Abby_Donovan: Goodnight Wilson (except Wilson is a lot nicer than you)

MarkBaynard: Goodnight Cameron

Abby_Donovan: Goodnight Foreman

MarkBaynard: Goodnight 13 (who is in no way hotter than you)

Abby_Donovan: Goodnight Chase

MarkBaynard: Goodnight Tweetheart...

Tuesday, June 7—1:56 P.M.

MarkBaynard: What are you wearing?

Abby_Donovan: Rizzo's Pink Lady jacket from GREASE over Kate Beckinsale's black leather catsuit from UNDERWORLD.

MarkBaynard: Mrrrrreow!

Abby_Donovan: Why do men love those UNDERWORLD movies so much?

MarkBaynard: I don't know, but I'm sure it has absolutely nothing to do with the way Kate Beckinsale looked in that catsuit.

Abby_Donovan: So what are YOU wearing?

MarkBaynard: John Wayne's tweed hat from THE QUIET MAN and the smile the automatic pilot was wearing at the end of AIRPLANE.

Abby_Donovan: I was too self-obsessed to ask where in the world Mark Baynard was the last time we tweeted.

MarkBaynard: VIEW FROM MY iPHONE: http://twitphoto.com/MB7sth

Abby_Donovan: Oh! OH!!! Tell me that's not...

MarkBaynard: I'm sitting at the top of Blarney Castle in County Cork, trying to find the words to describe a green that's utterly indescribable.

Abby_Donovan: You won't even have to kiss the Blarney Stone since you already have the gift of gab. Or at least the gift of tweet.

MarkBaynard: So how is the writing going today?

Abby_Donovan: VIEW FROM MY LAPTOP: http://tweetpic.com/2825190614

MarkBaynard: Am I seeing what I think I'm seeing? Are those the two most beautiful words in the English language—CHAPTER SIX?

Abby_Donovan: No, the two most beautiful words would be THE END. But this is a start. Especially since I've already written 15 pages to go with them.

MarkBaynard: Filled with your usual sparkling wit and sartorial brilliance, no doubt?

Abby_Donovan: Oh no. I took your advice. They're a total load of crap.

MarkBaynard: I've never been so proud to be your muse!

Abby_Donovan: Is that what you are? I thought you were my nemesis.

MarkBaynard: Salieri to your Mozart!

Abby_Donovan: Moriarty to my Sherlock Holmes!

MarkBaynard: Prince John to those two brats in the tower!

Abby_Donovan: The Sheriff of Nottingham to my Robin Hood!

MarkBaynard: Blofeld to your James Bond!

Abby_Donovan: Dr. Evil to my Austin Powers!

MarkBaynard: Donald Trump to your Joan Rivers!

Abby_Donovan: Kanye West to my Taylor Swift!

MarkBaynard: Joker to your Batman! Have you been chained to the computer since last we tweeted? Because I'm enjoying that image way more than I should.

Abby_Donovan: Oddly enough, writing again has made me WANT to get out more. I mean, if I don't start living life, how can I write about it?

MarkBaynard: Doubled our trips to Starbucks, have we?

Abby_Donovan: I'll have you know I actually volunteered at a charity event for juvenile diabetes in the park on Thursday.

MarkBaynard: Was there a Biff the Bunny suit involved?

Abby_Donovan: Worse. I was assigned to man the Giant Balloon Bouncer.

MarkBaynard: That big inflatable castle that sucks unsuspecting children to their doom?

Abby_Donovan: Shudder! It's a more ruthless exercise in "Survival of the Fittest" than 8th grade dodgeball.

MarkBaynard: If a 2-year-old can't survive a 5th grader jumping up & down on their spleen, they're not going to be of much use to society anyway, right?

Abby_Donovan: Exactly. At least they only peed on each other this time, not on me.

MarkBaynard: I always consider that a good day.

Abby_Donovan: Would your Dylan have survived?

MarkBaynard: I've already taught him how to bite the bigger kids in the ankle. After he takes them down with a karate chop to the groin.

Abby_Donovan: Tell me about him.

MarkBaynard: Well, he's three and a half years

old going on Peter Boyle in EVERYBODY LOVES RAYMOND.

Abby_Donovan: Is he as precocious as his father?

MarkBaynard: More so. Last time I saw him he was kicked back in the La-Z-Boy reading the Harvard Lampoon and chain-smoking unfiltered Camels.

Abby_Donovan: My God, he IS your son, isn't he?

MarkBaynard: His hobbies include long walks on the beach, eating all the marshmallows out of my Lucky Charms...

MarkBaynard: ...and making truck noises that involve a lot of spittle.

Abby_Donovan: He sounds like quite the handful.

MarkBaynard: He is, but I still can't bear to spank him.

Abby_Donovan: How do you discipline him then? Take away his Penthouse collection?

MarkBaynard: When he acts up, I just sit him on top of the refrigerator. By the time he climbs down, I've forgotten why I'm mad.

Abby_Donovan: Does he look like you?

MarkBaynard: He's no Mini-Me but he did inherit my hopelessly curly hair. Poor kid.

Abby_Donovan: You miss him, don't you?

MarkBaynard: With my every breath.

Abby_Donovan: How long have you been out of the States?

MarkBaynard: A little bit longer than I originally planned.

Abby_Donovan: When are you coming back?

MarkBaynard: My trip is a little open-ended at the moment.

Abby_Donovan: Don't you have to be back for the fall semester?

MarkBaynard: Only if I want to keep my job.

Abby_Donovan: I thought tenure meant never having to say you're sorry. Or unemployed.

MarkBaynard: It's called a sabbatical for a reason. If it goes on for more than a year, they change the name to "terminated"...

MarkBaynard: Well, that's enough foreplay for one day. I was wondering if you'd like to go on a second date?

Abby_Donovan: Even if I didn't put out on the first one?

MarkBaynard: Your nefarious ploy to trick me into asking you out again obviously worked. With luck, maybe I can get halfway to 1st base again.

Abby_Donovan: You're on. So where do you

want to go this time? Is Def Leprechaun playing down at the local pub?

MarkBaynard: I thought I'd come to you this time. Ladies' choice.

Abby_Donovan: All right, you can pick me up in front of the Plaza on Sunday morning at 10 a.m.

MarkBaynard: Where are we going? Mass?

Abby_Donovan: Sort of.

MarkBaynard: Did I ever tell you that I'm afraid of nuns? Even naughty ones?

Abby_Donovan: Well, drats. I'd better take the habit, the fishnet stockings, and the wooden ruler back to the costume store.

MarkBaynard: You're a shameless tease, you know. It's one of the things I love the most about you.

Abby_Donovan: And you're a shameless flirt.

MarkBaynard: That's where you're wrong. I'm blushing even as we speak.

Abby_Donovan: Goodnight Captain Peacock

MarkBaynard: Goodnight Mrs. Slocombe

Abby_Donovan: Drats! I just knew I was going to get you with that one! I'm never going to be able to stump you, am I?

MarkBaynard: What can I say? I'm a big PBS supporter. Plus DR. WHO got me addicted to BBC America.

Abby_Donovan: Goodnight Mr. Humphries
MarkBaynard: Goodnight Miss Brahms
Abby_Donovan: Goodnight Mr. Grainger
MarkBaynard: Goodnight Miss Belfridge
Abby_Donovan: Goodnight Young Mr. Grace
MarkBaynard: Goodnight Tweetheart…

Chapter Ten

Sunday, June 12—10:02 A.M.

MarkBaynard: What are you wearing?

   Abby_Donovan: Faded Levi's, an oversize blue men's shirt & a pair of red Chuck Taylors with my right pinkie toe peeking out of a hole in the top.

   MarkBaynard: That's the hottest thing I've ever heard. It's what you're really wearing, isn't it?

   Abby_Donovan: Well, I left off the Lance Armstrong LIVE STRONG wristband and the velvet scrunchie that went out of style in 1999, but yes. You?

   MarkBaynard: Rumpled chinos & a WHO'S YOUR PADDY? T-shirt I picked up in the pub last night. I think it was last night. It's all one big green blur.

   Abby_Donovan: Swillin' a wee bit too much o' the Guinness, are we, laddie?

   MarkBaynard: That would depend on whether

or not you consider leprechaun tossing a legitimate sport. Or cookie tossing.

Abby_Donovan: I heard they were thinking about adding them to the next Olympics.

MarkBaynard: They wouldn't be as exciting as curling.

Abby_Donovan: We couldn't have picked a more perfect day for our outing. The sun is shining. The sky is a dazzling blue. The birds are singing.

MarkBaynard: Would you mind asking them to tone it down? There's a chance my head might explode like that guy's in SCANNERS. So where are we headed?

Abby_Donovan: http://tweetpic.com/2825190615

MarkBaynard: It's the Poet's Walk in the park, isn't it? You were right. It does look like a cathedral.

Abby_Donovan: I pick up my coffee and come here every Sunday morning. In the snow. In the rain. And on perfect summer days like this one.

MarkBaynard: Tell me what you see right now.

Abby_Donovan: There's an old man walking his Russian wolfhound & a radiant Asian bride dressed in Vera Wang getting photos made for her wedding album...

Abby_Donovan: A couple sharing an ice cream cone and a little boy dragging his mom toward Bethesda Terrace...

Abby_Donovan: A man with a silver cart selling warm pretzels and an art student sipping a latte while he sketches one of the old oaks...

Abby_Donovan: That's what I love the most about the park on a Sunday morning. Even the people who are alone seem happy.

MarkBaynard: Are you happy?

Abby_Donovan: I don't think I was when we first met. But I am now.

MarkBaynard: Do you mind if I take your hand while we walk?

Abby_Donovan: Such a gentleman!

MarkBaynard: Well, it's not like we can walk and make out at the same time.

Abby_Donovan: And so practical!

MarkBaynard: I bet you say that to all the guys you drag to the park on a Sunday morning.

Abby_Donovan: If you must know, I've never taken anyone else here before. Well...except for my friend Margo.

MarkBaynard: I'm honored.

Abby_Donovan: What? No mockery? No sarcastic asides?

MarkBaynard: Witty bons mots no longer trip from my tongue. Your charms have undone me. Irony has deserted me.

Abby_Donovan: Are you being ironic?

MarkBaynard: Maybe I've simply fallen beneath the spell of this enchanted woodland.

Abby_Donovan: I like to think of it as one of the places I keep myself. That way if I ever lose myself, I'll know where to go back and find me.

MarkBaynard: What if you can't remember where you were when you lost yourself? What if it's too late to go back and look?

Abby_Donovan: It's never too late. As Cicero said, "As long as there's life, there's hope."

MarkBaynard: I thought that was John Lennon. But either way, they're both dead, aren't they?

Abby_Donovan: Maybe they were both wrong. Maybe hope never dies, not even when we do.

MarkBaynard: Now that is a philosophy I could embrace.

Abby_Donovan: So if we're not going to make out, what are we supposed to do on our second tweet date?

MarkBaynard: I believe this is the date where we start to explore what we're looking for in a relationship. While pretending we're not, of course.

Abby_Donovan: Wouldn't making out be less complicated?

MarkBaynard: Probably. So in the interest of subtlety...what exactly ARE you looking for in a man, Abigail Donovan?

Abby_Donovan: Hmm...well, he can be deeply flawed as long as he's willing to rush into a burning building to rescue a basket of kittens.

MarkBaynard: Is that smoke I smell? Wait right here...I'll be back!

Abby_Donovan: Mark?

Abby_Donovan: Um...Mark? Where did you go?

MarkBaynard: I'm back! Here, would you hold this basket for me while I brush the ashes out of my hair. Just ignore any plaintive mewing you might hear.

Abby_Donovan: Um...Mark...these aren't kittens. I think they might be ferrets. Angry ferrets. Angry rabid ferrets.

MarkBaynard: Hang on...I'll give them to the guy over there by the tree wearing the PETARF T-shirt.

Abby_Donovan: PETARF?

MarkBaynard: People for the Ethical Treatment of Angry Rabid Ferrets. There...now what were we talking about? Ow! Poor bastard! That's gonna leave a mark.

Abby_Donovan: I believe I was about to ask you (with equal subtlety) what you were looking for in a woman.

MarkBaynard: Someone to laugh with me. Or at me. Really...I'm not picky.

Abby_Donovan: So you're not looking for some sort of mythical soul mate?

MarkBaynard: I survived a rather acrimonious divorce. I'd settle for someone with a soul.

Abby_Donovan: Don't U want someone to complete you the way Mini-Me completed Dr. Evil? Someone who shares the same tastes in music & food who will finish

MarkBaynard:...my sentences? The last thing I need is someone stealing the punch lines to all my jokes.

Abby_Donovan: Did you believe your wife was your soul mate when you married her?

MarkBaynard: I was 22. I believed in rainbows, fairies, and My Little Pony. Hell, I believed Ricky Martin was straight.

Abby_Donovan: So what really happened between the two of you? Ten years is a long time to be married. Did you fall out of love?

MarkBaynard: No, we fell out of like. Which in the long run is a lot more damaging.

Abby_Donovan: I know couples that have been married 40 years who can barely stand to be in the same room together.

MarkBaynard: That's exactly why they're still married. Loathing is a form of passion. It's apathy that kills a relationship.

Abby_Donovan: Do you think you'll ever re-marry?

MarkBaynard: No.

Abby_Donovan: Wow...it really hurt when you found out My Little Pony wasn't real, didn't it?

MarkBaynard: It was the Ricky Martin thing that pushed me over the edge. Favorite divorce movie?

Abby_Donovan: STARTING OVER with Burt Reynolds and Jill Clayburgh.

MarkBaynard: THE WAR OF THE ROSES with Michael Douglas and Kathleen Turner. And yes, I know exactly what that says about me and it's not pretty.

Abby_Donovan: I love those old movies where women discover they can be happy without a man: IT'S MY TURN, MY BRILLIANT CAREER, AN UNMARRIED WOMAN.

MarkBaynard: You do know that nothing will make some poor sucker propose faster than telling him you believe you can be happy without a man?

Abby_Donovan: Men do love the thrill of the hunt, don't they?

MarkBaynard: Anything to throw another Barbie on the shrimp. Wait...maybe "shrimp" was a bad choice of words.

Abby_Donovan: What did you like the most about being married?

MarkBaynard: Having someone to hold when I woke up in the middle of the night.

Abby_Donovan: Just last night I woke to the delicious sensation of someone licking my ear.

MarkBaynard: Oh really? Do tell. I think I'm getting jealous.

Abby_Donovan: I giggled and felt all romantic...until I realized it was Willow Tum-Tum.

MarkBaynard: Went straight for the ear canal, eh? She was probably preparing to suck out your brain.

Abby_Donovan: Yes, I could hear Buffy the Mouse Slayer in the corner chanting, "Brains... BRAINS!!!"

MarkBaynard: I'm guessing any man wanting to lick your ear in the middle of the night would have to be a cat person.

Abby_Donovan: I like dogs, but I do love cats. It's probably unfair, but I always assume people who have cats are good people.

MarkBaynard: Unless they're having them for dinner.

Abby_Donovan: Ew!

MarkBaynard: Sorry. I spent a summer in Malaysia once.

Abby_Donovan: Sex slave?

MarkBaynard: They wouldn't have me so I had to settle for teaching English on a volunteer basis.

Abby_Donovan: I thought you didn't believe in giving it away for free?

MarkBaynard: The ability to conjugate verbs isn't quite as much in demand as the ability to mix them with nouns and adjectives to create a narrative.

Abby_Donovan: Spoken like a true English lit professor.

MarkBaynard: As opposed to a pompous windbag with as yet unrealized literary aspirations?

Abby_Donovan: You never have told me what you'd like to write about.

MarkBaynard: As soon as I figure it out, I promise you'll be the first to know.

Abby_Donovan: Will I? You might be tweeting up some other semi-agoraphobic washed-up writer by then.

MarkBaynard: Or you might have decided you deserve more than a quickie in the back of a cab where we exchange fake cell numbers afterward.

Abby_Donovan: I could always give you my real cell number.

Abby_Donovan: Mark?

Abby_Donovan: Mark? Was it something I said?

Abby_Donovan: Geez, I just offered you my cell phone number, not the number of a wedding planner.

MarkBaynard: Have you forgotten that I might be a serial killer?

Abby_Donovan: Or Ashton Kutcher. I'm much younger than Demi, you know, if not quite as well preserved.

MarkBaynard: I'm sorry. I didn't mean to hurt your feelings.

Abby_Donovan: You could have at least taken the number & pretended you were going to call. That's what any self-respecting jerk would have done.

MarkBaynard: What if I don't respect myself?

Abby_Donovan: Unless you really are in Witness Protection, you might be carrying this International Man of Mystery schtick a little too far.

MarkBaynard: I promise you there's nothing I'd like more in this entire world than to hear your voice…

MarkBaynard: I just don't want to do it through a cell phone. I'd rather wait until we can meet face-to-face.

Abby_Donovan: What are you suggesting?

That we make a pact to meet a year from now at the top of the Empire State Building?

MarkBaynard: I'm afraid of heights. How about the basement of Macy's?

Abby_Donovan: Oh goody, they might be having a sale!

MarkBaynard: I thought you didn't like shopping. Or clothes.

Abby_Donovan: But I do like sales.

MarkBaynard: It's a date then. (I gently cup your face in my hands and kiss you like the first time Sawyer kissed Kate on LOST.)

MarkBaynard: Abby...are you still there?

Abby_Donovan: I do believe you've left me tweetless.

MarkBaynard: Who knew that was even possible? Goodnight Mrs. Huxtable

Abby_Donovan: Goodnight Theo

MarkBaynard: Goodnight Rudy

Abby_Donovan: Goodnight Dr. Huxtable

MarkBaynard: Goodnight Vanessa

Abby_Donovan: Goodnight Elvin

MarkBaynard: Goodnight Tweetheart...

Chapter Eleven

No matter how old a girl got, there would always be days when she needed her mom. And Abby was wise enough to know the Sunday after her second "date" with Mark was one of those days. Since they couldn't dish over frozen hot chocolates at Serendipity or go on a shopping binge at Bergdorf, Abby did the next best thing. She took the subway to the Bronx and trudged the mile and a half in the sweltering summer heat to the nursing care facility where her mom lived.

Any fantasy Abby and her dad had entertained about caring for her mom at home had died the morning her dad had walked into the sunny kitchen of their house to find her mom about to mix up a blender full of Drāno daiquiris. After his death, Abby had transferred her mom from the nursing home in North Carolina to Sunshine Manor—a five star–rated facility that specialized in the treatment of patients with Alzheimer's and other forms of early-onset dementia.

She punched a four-digit code into the keypad next to the triple-paned glass door of the non-descript brick building. The door swung open, buffeting Abby with a rush of stale air-conditioning. The hallway in front of her seemed to stretch off into infinity, forcing her to run a gauntlet of parked wheelchairs and roaming residents before she reached her mother's room. Most of the residents had stopped having visitors a long time ago, so each new arrival was greeted with a heartbreaking mixture of hope and resignation.

"Are you my daughter?" one woman asked plaintively, her white head bobbing up and down like a child's toy lost at sea.

Abby paused long enough to give the woman's outstretched hand a squeeze. "No, Elsie. Don't you remember? I'm Brenda's daughter."

"Get over here and help me with my wheel-chair, young lady," demanded a striking black woman with a grizzled short-cropped Afro and one leg. "It's stuck."

Abby squatted to adjust the wheelchair brake before moving on.

A shrunken little old man tottered up to her. "Could you take me to the bathroom, please?" A covert glance at the front of his pants showed that his request had come a few seconds too late.

"I'm not allowed to do that, Mr. Dugan, but I'll tell one of the nurses to come help you when I go by the desk."

In the two years she'd been visiting the nursing facility, Abby had discovered it took very little to make the residents happy—a smile, a hug, an encouraging word. Some acknowledgment of their existence that went beyond helping them into their pajamas or doling out medications. The nursing staff was incredibly caring, yet desperately harried as they dealt with cutbacks and shortages and the inevitable burnout that went hand in hand with caring for those who could no longer care for themselves.

After sending a patient aide to rescue poor Mr. Dugan, Abby slipped into the room directly across from the nursing station. Her mother was sound asleep in her lift recliner, her chin resting on her chest. On the flat screen of the television mounted on the opposite wall, a muted Lucy Ricardo was dragging a handcuffed Ricky through a nightclub decorated with fake palm trees.

Her mom's spacious private room was as homey as Abby could make it. She had brightened the generic blandness of the wheat-colored walls and sturdy oak furniture by adding whimsical touches, such as the large Shrek pillow doll perched on the hospital bed and the framed poster of a leering Johnny Depp as Captain Jack Sparrow hanging over the dresser. The bookshelves were lined with DVDs of animated Disney movies and every romantic comedy ever made featuring Julia Roberts or Sandra Bullock.

Her mom had always been prone to losing her mind, but with the help of Abby's dad she had usually been able to find it again. It wasn't irretrievably lost until a severe reaction to her medications had resulted in early-onset dementia, making it impossible to treat her bipolar disorder with the usual cocktail of lithium and whatever psychotropic drug was currently in fashion. Since her first major manic episode had occurred right after Abby was born when her postpartum hormones were in hyperdrive, Abby had the genuine—if dubious—distinction of knowing her first act in life had been to drive another human being stark raving mad.

Abby leaned down to press a kiss to the softness of her mother's cheek. No matter how diligent the nursing staff, it was still a shock to Abby's senses when her mom smelled faintly of pee instead of the Chanel No. 5 talcum powder Abby's dad had given her every Christmas. "Hey, sweetie," Abby said softly, trying not to startle her. "How's my best girl today?"

In the past few years their roles seemed to have reversed, leaving Abby feeling less like a daughter and more like the mother of a frequently charming but occasionally unmanageable toddler.

Her mom lifted her head and blinked at Abby. "Hey, baby," she said, offering Abby a sleepy little smile.

Abby straightened, breathing a silent sigh of relief. Her mom's dark green eyes were a little glazed, but there was no trace of suspicion or hostility in them. She was apparently having one of her "quiet" days.

Abby pulled a Ziploc bag of makeup out of her purse with a bold flourish. "Are you ready for your close-up?"

Although Abby's own makeup usually consisted of a hastily applied splotch of blush to each cheek and a dab of clear lip gloss, her mom had always been one of those women who refused to leave the house without a full complement of liquid eyeliner. At this point there wasn't much Abby could do to help her, but she could at least make sure she recognized the woman staring back at her from the bathroom mirror.

Her mother sat like a china doll while Abby smoothed moisturizer on her cheeks, then followed up with a layer of foundation.

At fifty-four her mom was one of the youngest residents in the facility. Spending the last four years out of the sun had left her face eerily unlined. Her mink brown hair was only lightly streaked with gray and pulled back in a bouncy ponytail that made her look like a slightly overweight, middle-aged Gidget. Abby's dad used to joke that her mom was like Dorian Gray. Instead of having a rapidly aging portrait tucked away in some attic, she had him.

Now that he was gone, Abby supposed she would have to be her mother's portrait. She would have to measure the passing moments of her mother's life by the wrinkles and worry lines etched on her own skin.

Almost as if reading Abby's thoughts, her mom suddenly said, "I'm so glad you're here. Your daddy is coming this afternoon. He should be here anytime."

Although the words made her heart flinch, Abby kept her smile carefully plastered in place. When Abby had been forced to tell her mother a sudden stroke had felled the man who had been a larger-than-life hero to them both, she had thought it was the worst day of her life. But the worst day had turned out to be the one after that when Abby had arrived at the nursing home, her eyes still so swollen from crying she could barely see, only to discover her mother had forgotten their entire conversation.

She had turned her hopeful face to Abby and said, "Is your daddy with you? He always comes on Thursdays."

Once again Abby had been forced to break her mother's heart. Once again her mother had collapsed in her arms and sobbed like a child who had lost both father and mother. The pattern had continued for nearly a week until an exhausted and emotionally battered Abby had finally decided that neither one of them was going to survive another day of reliving such grief.

Now her mother seemed perfectly content to tell everyone who would listen that Abby's daddy was coming. It didn't seem to bother her that he never arrived. Maybe it was less painful for her to spend the rest of her life waiting for him than to admit he was never coming back.

Abby used her pinkie to apply a lavender tint to her mother's delicate eyelids. "I've met somebody of my own, Mama."

"Elvis? Did you meet Elvis?"

"Nope. Elvis is still at Graceland with Priscilla and Lisa Marie. My guy's name is Mark. And I think he might like me."

"Is he going to ask you to the homecoming dance?"

Abby felt a small, secret smile play around her mouth. "Maybe. Do you think I should go if he does?"

Her mother frowned as if seriously considering the idea. "Is this boy trustworthy? I don't want you dating anybody you can't trust. I never did like you chasing after those bad boys."

Abby's smile vanished as she remembered how abruptly Mark had backed off when she had offered him her phone number. But then he had sworn there was nothing in the entire world he'd rather do than hear her voice. He had claimed that he wanted to meet her face-to-face for the first time, not through the impersonal circuits of a cell phone. And he had kissed her the way Sawyer kissed Kate for the first time on *Lost*.

Laying aside the bag of makeup, she sank down on her mother's bed, checking out of habit to make sure it was dry first. "I don't know if I can trust him yet. All I know is that he makes me happy. I'm getting out more. I'm writing again. I decided to take his advice and write what I *don't* know. He was right all along. I may have only been given one life to live, but that doesn't mean I've only been given one story to tell."

Her mother's eyes were already beginning to drift shut. Her chin bobbed toward her chest.

Abby's voice faded as she realized she was talking to herself once again. Maybe she'd always been talking to herself. "Even if he was trustworthy, I'm not sure I could trust him." She tilted her head to study her mother's sleeping face, her heart awash with helpless love and guilt. She had no desire to prolong her mother's suffering, but she was already selfishly dreading the day when she could no longer walk into this room and rest her head against the softness of her mother's shoulder like a little girl seeking comfort after a bad dream. "I'm not sure I can ever trust anybody, Mama," Abby whispered. "First you left me. Then Daddy left me."

Her mother lifted her head and looked directly at Abby, her eyes shining with a childlike faith that reminded Abby of summer picnics and Christmas mornings. "Your daddy didn't leave you, baby. He'll be here in just a little while."

Chapter Twelve

Monday, June 13—7:59 P.M.

*M*arkBaynard: Abby? We need to talk.

Abby_Donovan: Aren't those the four most dreaded words a man can hear from a woman?

MarkBaynard: Maybe that's why I'm saying them first.

Abby_Donovan: You're breaking up with me, aren't you? You've found some other woman on Twitter with a hotter, wetter tongue.

MarkBaynard: Look...I know I'm incapable of sounding serious, but I'm being serious this time. Dead serious.

Abby_Donovan: Good. Because I need to talk to you too. Seriously.

MarkBaynard: Please let me say what I have to say first.

Abby_Donovan: I thought it was always ladies first? Or is that only on the TITANIC?

MarkBaynard: An apt metaphor, I'm afraid. I've been thinking about this—and you—every minute of the day ever since you offered me your cell phone number.

Abby_Donovan: Okay, now you're really starting to scare me. Don't you want to know what I'm wearing? Or not wearing?

MarkBaynard: Ask me where in the world I am today.

Abby_Donovan: Huh?

MarkBaynard: Just do it. Ask me where I am today.

Abby_Donovan: O-o-o-o-okie dokie. Where in the world is Mark Baynard today?

MarkBaynard: VIEW FROM MY iPHONE: http://twitphoto.com/MB7sti

Abby_Donovan: I can't tell what that is. It looks like a piece of wood. And what's that bag on the pole and that thing with the lights?

MarkBaynard: It's the footboard of my hospital bed. The bag is full of IV fluids and meds and that thing with the lights is a monitor.

Abby_Donovan: Oh Mark, what happened? Are you okay?

MarkBaynard: No. I'm not okay. And I never was.

Abby_Donovan: I don't understand.

MarkBaynard: You've been right about me from the very beginning. I'm an imposter.

Abby_Donovan: So you really ARE Batman?

MarkBaynard: No, I'm really Mark Baynard, English lit professor on sabbatical from Ole Miss. But the only place I've traveled in the past year...

MarkBaynard:...is to a facility that specializes in experimental treatments for non-Hodgkins lymphoma.

Abby_Donovan: Lymphoma? As in...cancer?

MarkBaynard: I'm afraid so. I beat it as a teenager, but it recurred a couple of years ago when I turned 33.

Abby_Donovan: I've always heard non-Hodgkins lymphoma was one of the most treatable kinds of cancer.

MarkBaynard: It can be.

Abby_Donovan: What are you trying to say?

MarkBaynard: That you can't always believe what you hear.

Abby_Donovan: That's becoming painfully obvious. So let me get this straight—there was never any Paris? No Tuscany? No Loire Valley?

MarkBaynard: No. Just me sitting in this hospital room with my laptop in semi-isolation waiting for the mad scientists to come and harvest my stem cells.

Abby_Donovan: What about all the pictures you sent? The Eiffel Tower? Neptune's Fountain? Blarney Castle?

MarkBaynard: Just .jpgs I pulled off the Internet of the places I never took the time to see before I relapsed.

Abby_Donovan: So our entire relationship, such as it was, has been based on a lie.

MarkBaynard: And some of the most profound truths I've ever shared with anyone. I just left out the parts about the chemo and the vomiting.

Abby_Donovan: Why? Why would you do such a thing? Did you think I wouldn't be able to handle it?

MarkBaynard: It wasn't your problem. Why should you have to handle it?

Abby_Donovan: You could have trusted me enough to let me make that decision for myself. You didn't have to lie to me.

MarkBaynard: I wasn't just lying to you. I was lying to myself...

MarkBaynard:...I wanted to pretend it wasn't too late to travel to all the romantic places I'd always dreamed of seeing...

MarkBaynard:...to believe I might actually start that novel I've been plotting in the back of my brain since I graduated from college...

MarkBaynard:...to flirt with a smart, funny, irresistible woman.

Abby_Donovan: You left off stupid and gullible.

MarkBaynard: I never saw you that way. Not for one tweet.

Abby_Donovan: You let me drone on & on about my pathetic case of writer's block while you were fighting for yr life? How do you think that makes me feel?

MarkBaynard: At the moment I'm guessing really pissed off. But "fighting" might be too strong of a word. It was more like swinging wildly.

MarkBaynard: Abby?

MarkBaynard: Say something, Abby. Anything.

MarkBaynard: I'm guessing you only have two words for me right now. And they're not "Br*tney Sp*ars."

MarkBaynard: And I'm guessing only one of them is FCC-approved.

MarkBaynard: I was a bastard & I don't blame you for hating me. You're entitled to throw the mother of all Twantrums. But don't shut me out. Please.

MarkBaynard: Abby?

MarkBaynard: Tweetheart?

Abby_Donovan: #MarkFAIL

#

The laptop's hard drive whirred to a halt. Abby gently closed the screen, her fingers numb. For the first time she regretted getting the laptop with the stainless-steel casing. She wanted to slam the screen repeatedly on the keyboard until there was nothing left but shattered fragments of glass and plastic. She wanted to pick up the hateful thing and hurl it through the window, to send it crashing down onto Fifth Avenue with an impact that would bring the whole world screeching to a halt, along with her heart.

What did it matter if Mark had lied? Or even if he died? He was nothing to her. Just some stranger she'd been foolish enough to pick up on the Internet. He was no more real than the actors on the front of the tabloids down at the local bodega. No more real than Mr. Darcy looking down his gorgeously aristocratic nose at Elizabeth Bennett from the lofty edifice of his pride.

The intimacy they'd shared was nothing but a carefully crafted illusion. The nonsense of their little rituals. Their silly inside jokes. The secrets they'd traded. Their imaginary dates. Their ridiculous plan to meet in the basement of Macy's a year from now.

None of it was real. *He* wasn't real.

Why should it matter to her if he'd sent his tweets from some lonely hospital bed instead of from a sunny Tuscan vineyard halfway across the world? Why should she care if he lay awake until the wee hours of the morning watching endless re-runs of *The Golden Girls* because it was better than listening to the monitors count out each beat of his heart and wondering just how many were left?

She reached up to scrub at her cheeks, surprised to find them wet. She couldn't remember the last time she had cried. Her tears seemed to have dried up during that awful week when she had been forced to break the news of her father's death to her mother over and over again.

Willow Tum-Tum brushed up against her leg with that peculiar empathy some cats seemed to possess, while Buffy eyed her with dispassionate curiosity from the ottoman in front of the couch.

She glared at the laptop through her tears. Even with it silenced, she could still hear Mark's voice:

I'm just not convinced the poor schlub who ends his life puking his guts out in a hospital trash can would agree with you.

Life has meaning simply because it's . . . life. You don't have to go out and wrap your BMW around a tree to find the value in it.

There are meaningful deaths. And there are absurd

and utterly meaningless deaths. Unfortunately, you don't get to choose which one you get.

In a John Irving novel, nobody ever dies a meaningless death.

Death of choice? Choking to death on a Krispy Kreme.

She shoved herself away from the desk and began to pace the length of the long, narrow apartment. She wished for the very first time that she had sublet some spacious Soho loft. Never had her apartment seemed like nothing more than the renovated hotel room it was. The tastefully painted walls seemed to be closing in around her. She could only seem to breathe in ragged gulps that made her heart feel as if it were going to explode from her chest. The shadows of twilight began to fall outside the window, crowding the last of the daylight from the room and turning the city streets below into gloomy tunnels.

She tore open the door of the SubZero refrigerator. All it took was a quick survey of its contents to realize this was a wound no amount of Ben & Jerry's could heal.

She let the door fall shut and rested her throbbing forehead against the cool stainless steel. She could almost feel the laptop behind her, crouched there in the dark like some living, breathing creature. No longer able to stand its mute reproach, she snatched up her wallet and keys and fled the apartment.

Abby would have liked nothing more than to dart across Grand Army Plaza and disappear into the shadows of the park to lick her wounds. But even in her agitated state, she knew that walking alone in the park after dark was an invitation for her unsolved mugging, rape, or murder to be ripped from the headlines and featured on an episode of *Law & Order* or *CSI: New York*. So she turned left and took off down Fifth Avenue, shoving her way through the bustling crowds of theatergoers headed for the garish lights of Times Square.

The vast and varied population of the city was both its blessing and its curse. The freedom of anonymity could be intoxicating until the moment when you realized you were surrounded by millions of people and not one of them gave a damn whether you lived or died.

As she passed the artfully lighted windows of Saks, the ghostly white mannequins in their designer dresses looked down on her with equal apathy, as if to say, "We have nipples, but no need of them. We will never know your pain."

Full dark fell as she walked. The lights of the

city twinkled to life around her, as cold and distant as stars from another galaxy. She walked until she could feel the pavement through the thin soles of her flats. She awoke from her daze to realize she was several blocks past Times Square and both the crowds and the lights had begun to thin.

Leery of venturing deeper into a part of the city she didn't know, she ducked into the nearest subway station.

The subway car she picked was nearly deserted except for an elderly woman wearing a babushka, a weary-looking businessman reading *The Wall Street Journal* on his iPad, and a pair of giggling teenagers dressed all in black with nearly every visible inch of their sun-deprived flesh either tattooed or pierced. Abby sank into one of the cheap plastic seats at the back of the car. Breathing in the all too familiar smell of stale sweat mingled with various other mercifully unidentifiable odors, she closed her eyes and gave herself over to the rocking rhythm of the train. When she opened them again, the train was arriving at the Franklin Street subway station.

She emerged from the station at the corner of Franklin and Varick in the very heart of Tribeca. She supposed she had known where she had been going all along. She had spent the two years since her father's death convincing herself that she didn't need anybody. That her work and the vibrant heartbeat of the city would be enough to sustain her. But then Mark had come along at the worst possible time and proved her wrong.

She had forgotten to grab her cell phone when fleeing the apartment so she had no choice but to cast herself on the mercy of the liveried doorman standing guard at the revolving glass doors of the luxury high-rise. With her uncombed hair and wild, red-rimmed eyes, she probably looked like some Greenwich Village crack addict who had stumbled off the train at the wrong stop. If the doorman hadn't remembered her from past visits, he would have never let her into the building.

Before she had time to catch her breath, an express elevator had whisked her up to the thirty-seventh floor. Feeling like a beggar at the gates, she banged on the door at the far end of the hall, already knowing that the odds of anyone actually being home ranged from slim to none.

It was almost a shock when the door swung open to reveal Margo standing there in a short scarlet silk robe screened with an Asian print. Her feet were bare but her hair was still perfectly coiffed. The most gorgeous Hispanic man Abby had ever seen hovered in the doorway of the bedroom behind her, wearing nothing but a towel and a disgruntled expression.

Margo's face lit up when she saw Abby. "There you are, baby! I thought you were coming by in the morning." Before Abby could say a word, she turned away and padded across the granite tiles to the sleek steel-and-glass desk sitting beneath the low-slung bank of windows. She rapidly shuffled her way through several file folders with her long crimson nails. "Lucky for you, I picked up the ticket on my way home from the office. At first I didn't think they were going to let me transfer over my frequent flier miles, but by the time I was done with the airline rep, he was begging to upgrade me—I mean, *you*—to first class. Ah, here it is! I still think you're a little crazy jetting halfway across the world to meet a man who might be the next Ted Bundy, but hey, at least it'll get you out of the apartment for a few days, right? And I have to tell you, I don't mind feeding those furry little monsters of yours while you're gone, but that shifty little Muffy or Fluffy or Tuffy or whatever it is you call her still gives me the heebie jeebies."

Margo was halfway back across the room before she lifted her gaze from the printout in her hand and realized Abby hadn't budged from the doorway. She drew closer, her regal features going taut with concern as she searched Abby's face. "Abby? What happened, baby? Are you all right?"

Feeling fresh tears burn her eyes, Abby swiped at her dripping nose with the back of her hand. "I won't be needing that ticket after all, but I do need you to drop-kick somebody's lily-white ass to the moon for me. I'll let you be Oprah for an entire month if you won't say 'I told you so' or 'bless your little heart.'"

Her face crumpling in sympathy, Margo opened her arms. Abby fell into them with a choked sob, still not sure if she was crying for Mark or for herself.

Chapter Thirteen

atched the IQ episode of FRASIER last night. Learned I'm smarter than Frasier but dumber than Niles.

If I were president, I'd appoint a Starbucks czar, a hot stone massage czar, and a dark chocolate M&M's czar.

Doctors should give out bottles of Dark Choco M&M's labeled HAPPY PILLS. Take 30 and don't call me in the morning.

Dear New Age CD: This track might be more relaxing if it didn't sound just like the music they played when TITANIC was sinking.

Abby groaned out loud, earning a faintly annoyed look from the man skimming the *Times* and nursing a Caramel Macchiato at the next table. She was doing it again. Tweeting in her head. Collecting observations of 140 characters or less to share with Mark. She desperately wished there was some way she could flip the stubborn switch in her brain to Off so it would stop tweeting. It was almost as if it was sending out some sort of distress signal to a tower that was no longer receiving.

She took a sip of her latte, then grimaced. The coffee had grown stone cold while she sat absently watching the traffic pass by on Fifth Avenue and chatting up a phantom. Before she had "met" Mark, she hadn't wanted to leave her apartment. Now she only returned there to sleep. She just couldn't bear to be trapped in the same room with her laptop, much less think about actually turning it on. She'd let it sit cold, dark, and silent since she'd signed off of Twitter for the last time nearly a week ago.

During that week she had learned there were a lot of places in New York where you could loiter all day without being arrested for vagrancy—the public library, the Guggenheim, the Metropolitan Museum of Art, Rockefeller Center, St. Patrick's Cathedral. One sunny afternoon she had even laid claim to one of the benches that lined the Poet's Walk. But the sight of all the happy couples had driven her out of the park to wander the bustling streets until she was so exhausted she had no choice but to return to her apartment and fall into bed. She had slept all night without dreaming a single dream.

After that she had returned to her old familiar stomping ground. Fueled by caffeine and righteous indignation, she had been writing at various Starbucks all week, scrawling page after page of her new book on a yellow legal pad in her barely legible handwriting. Judging by the superior smirks of her fellow Starbucks customers, with their sleek iPads and vibrating BlackBerrys, you'd have thought she was using a chisel to carve her words into a stone tablet.

She might be able to escape her apartment and her laptop, but there was nowhere she could go to escape her own brain. She was still haunted by the ghost of a man who had never even really existed. She would have almost sworn they had actually strolled the Poet's Walk hand in hand while trading semi-serious quips about what they were looking for in a relationship.

Do you think you'll ever remarry?

No.

She might know the truth about Mark's medical condition, but she had no way of knowing if he had responded that way because his divorce had left his heart so badly scarred or because he didn't believe he would live long enough to marry again. He had lied to her with effortless charm, yet it was those heartbreaking moments of honesty she couldn't seem to forget.

She still couldn't believe she'd only been a tweet

away from revealing that she had already pur-
chased a ticket to Dublin. From telling him that her
mother's unwavering faith in love—a faith that
transcended even death—had inspired her to take
a chance. To tear down the walls she'd built around
her own heart, even if that meant risking everything by offering it to a man she barely knew.

But before she could do that, he had sent his
own wrecking ball crashing through them.

She didn't want to think about how difficult his
confession must have been for him or picture him
lying in that hospital bed the entire time they had
been tweeting. She couldn't afford to feel sorry for
him. She didn't have any room left in her heart to
grieve another loss. She wanted to hold on to her
anger for as long as she could. She was afraid of
what she might feel when she no longer had its jagged edges to protect her.

She scribbled another line on the yellow pad,
hoping to occupy her brain with something more
productive than brooding. A familiar chirp sounded
behind her. She froze, the cheery sound cutting
through her heart like a blade. She slowly turned to
look over her shoulder, as if fearful any sudden
move might sever some essential artery.

A twenty-something girl with a bright magenta
pashima draped over one shoulder had claimed

the high-top table behind her and flipped open her laptop to reveal Tweetdeck's distinctive columns. The laptop chirped again, signaling the arrival of another tweet. The girl grinned as she read it, then sent her fingers flying over the keys to craft a response.

Only a week ago that might have been her, Abby thought. But as she had discovered since that night when she had abandoned Mark in mid-tweet, a week could be an eternity.

Or it could be only the blink of an eye in the life of a man battling lymphoma.

Seized by a sudden rush of panic, Abby jumped to her feet and stuffed her legal pad into her portfolio with shaking hands. She started for the door, stumbling over the outstretched legs of the man nursing the Caramel Macchiato.

"I'm so sorry," she said, rushing past him as he gave her a disapproving glare over the top of his newspaper. "I'm so very, very sorry."

Abby stared at the screen of her laptop, hypnotized by the cheery yellow square with the silhouette of a blackbird perched in her dock. All she had to do was slide her cursor over it and click to open her Tweetdeck. She'd already taken the first step by turning the computer on.

She steadied her trembling fingers by closing them over her wireless mouse. Buffy and Willow Tum-Tum watched her every move from the foot of the futon she had called a bed for the past four years, managing to look both bored and expectant in the way that only cats could.

Outside the window the sun had already begun to set. Soon the room would be lit only by the intimate glow of the laptop. If Mark wasn't actually in Europe, then they might even be in the same time zone. He might be lying in some hospital bed, watching the day fade and wondering if she was doing the same.

Knowing there was only one way to find out, she gave the mouse a decisive tap with her index finger. Her neglected Tweetdeck sprang to life, its orderly row of columns filling the screen. At first it was completely blank. She didn't realize she was holding her breath until the first tweet popped up on the screen with a cheerful chirp, only to be quickly followed by a dizzying array of others.

She didn't even glance at them. She only had eyes for the empty column that was her Direct Message column. She closed those eyes briefly, her heart catching in her chest. When she opened them, the Direct Message column was full. Confused, she squinted at the column. All of the mes-

sages had come from the same person, but she
didn't recognize the profile pic. That's when she
realized Mark had changed his avatar from the generic Twitter bluebird to a .jpg of John Cusack
holding the boom box over his head as Lloyd
Dobler in *Say Anything*.

She cupped a hand over her mouth to capture a
sound halfway between a laugh and a sob.

Knowing it would be impossible to read anything but his most recent tweets on Tweetdeck, she
minimized the app and went directly to the Twitter website. Every Direct Message she'd ever received was still stored there. She had to track back
over five pages to find the date when she'd stormed
out of their cyber-playground with her day-of-the-
week panties in a wad.

Over twenty-four hours had passed before
Mark had dared to tweet again.

Tuesday, June 14—7:35 P.M.

MarkBaynard: I'm guessing you're listening to
WE USED TO BE FRIENDS by the Dandy Warhols
right about now. (You know—the theme from VE-
RONICA MARS.)

MarkBaynard: You haven't Unfollowed me or

Blocked me yet so I'm going to assume you're still receiving.

MarkBaynard: I want you to know that I don't blame you for blowing me off.

MarkBaynard: I won't even take it personally if you're wishing me dead at the moment. But I should warn you that it takes more than that to kill me.

MarkBaynard: My doctors have been trying to kill me since I was sixteen. They redoubled their efforts recently, but have still met with limited success.

MarkBaynard: So far they've only succeeded in making me WISH I was dead.

MarkBaynard: At least we still have that much in common. We both wish I was dead.

MarkBaynard: You're probably waiting for me to say I'm sorry. But I'm not and I'd be lying if I said I was.

MarkBaynard: And I figure you've had just about enough of me lying to you. The truth is you've been the only bright spot in some pretty dismal weeks.

MarkBaynard: If not for you, I never would have gotten to see the Eiffel Tower while sipping espresso in a Paris cafe.

MarkBaynard: I never would have watched the

sun set over the vineyards from a balcony in Tuscany.

MarkBaynard: I never would have listened to the cathedral bells echo through a piazza in Florence.

MarkBaynard: And I never would have kissed the Blarney Stone and wished for the words to tell you the truth.

MarkBaynard: So I'm not sorry I lied to you, but I am sorry for being such a selfish bastard about it.

MarkBaynard: In the interest of no longer being a selfish, lying bastard, I shall now own up to having non-Hodgkins lymphoma Stage III.

MarkBaynard: (As opposed to Stage Right, where they'll be expecting me to exit if this new experimental treatment doesn't work.)

MarkBaynard: I was diagnosed and underwent chemo and a bone marrow transplant for the first time when I was 16.

MarkBaynard: I stayed in remission for 17 years until the lymphoma decided to kick my ass again. I didn't respond as well to treatment this time around.

MarkBaynard: They've spent the past few months preparing to harvest my stem cells for a new experimental treatment.

MarkBaynard: This disease is a little like the

California penal system—three strikes and you're out.

MarkBaynard: At the moment the count is full with 2 strikes & 3 balls. But I decided it would be better to go down swinging than take a called 3rd strike.

MarkBaynard: Oh hell, here comes my nurse with my 8 p.m. meds: http://twitphoto.com/MB7stj

MarkBaynard: Are you too young to recognize Nurse Ratched? It's times like this that I really miss your Naughty Nurse costume.

MarkBaynard: And you.

MarkBaynard: Goodnight Tweetheart...

Wednesday, June 15—7:30 P.M.

MarkBaynard: I hope you're not disappointed to discover I'm still clinging to life.

MarkBaynard: Rough night last night. After Nurse Ratched and her magical mystery medications had their way with me, I was way too wired to sleep.

MarkBaynard: Only thing on TV was a KEEPING UP WITH THE KARDASHIANS marathon, which made me long even more keenly for the sweet oblivion of death.

MarkBaynard: So I downloaded a copy of A FINE AND PRIVATE PLACE and spent most of the night reading your favorite book.

MarkBaynard: If you'd told me it was about a guy who lives in a graveyard, a couple of ghosts & a snarky talking raven I'd have read it a long time ago.

MarkBaynard: The raven kind of reminded me of me. I like that in a talking bird.

MarkBaynard: I can't decide if the moral of the story is that love transcends death or death transcends love.

MarkBaynard: I have learned that nausea transcends both death & love. As do the powdered scrambled eggs they feed you for breakfast in this place.

MarkBaynard: Who even knew it was possible to be nauseated and starving to death all at the same time?

MarkBaynard: I was wondering if we could go to Cracker Barrel on our next date?

MarkBaynard: Maybe order up one of those big sampler platters w/eggs, biscuits and gravy, hash browns, apples, pancakes, warm maple syrup, muffins...

MarkBaynard:...and an entire pig brought straight to your table w/another pig in his mouth instead of an apple.

MarkBaynard: That's my sad little fantasy these days—you and a whole lot of bacon.

MarkBaynard: I could buy you something from the gift shop while we're there. Maybe some salt-water taffy or Patsy Cline's Greatest Hits.

MarkBaynard: Or one of those old-timey toys where you use that stick on a cord to try to get the magnetic shavings to stick to the bald guy's head.

MarkBaynard: Or a bubble gum cigar. I could slide the little paper ring from it onto your finger and we could make jokes about how cheap I am.

MarkBaynard: Of course if you're more of a Grand Slam from Denny's kind of gal, I understand.

MarkBaynard: They usually let me wear my own clothes except on days when I have to have more tests.

MarkBaynard: These hospital gowns give a whole new meaning to the phrase "full disclosure."

MarkBaynard: Today I accidentally mooned the grumpy old lady in the next room & an ultra-bitchy X-ray tech.

MarkBaynard: At least I pretended it was an accident.

MarkBaynard: Goodnight Tweetheart...

Thursday, June 16—3:47 P.M.

MarkBaynard: If it's revenge you're plotting, it should delight you to learn my mother breezed into town today for a visit. (Cue Darth Vader theme.)

MarkBaynard: Even after all these years of dealing with this disease, she still seems torn between fluffing my pillow and smothering me with it.

MarkBaynard: I can never tell if she's more disappointed in me for being inconsiderate enough to get sick again...

MarkBaynard:...or for not having expired in a more timely manner that wouldn't have interfered with her Monday night Bunko game.

MarkBaynard: I think she's always secretly believed there's no ailment a pack of Virginia Slims Lights and a 3-martini lunch can't cure.

MarkBaynard: Or a 3-Cosmo lunch since she got hooked on those SEX AND THE CITY DVDs my brother bought her last Christmas.

MarkBaynard: I can't begin to tell you how disturbingitwastohearheruse"absof*ckinglutely" in a sentence for the first time.

MarkBaynard: When I was in treatment as a teenager I was always afraid she'd show up at the hospital & accidentally drink 1 of my radioactive cocktails.

MarkBaynard: Did I ever tell you she tells everybody she's five years older than she is just so they'll say, "Wow! You look great for your age!"?

MarkBaynard: I'm going to start telling everyone I'm 75 so they'll think I look fabulous.

MarkBaynard: I'm guessing you're gleefully poking pins in your Mark Baynard voodoo doll right now bcuz here comes another vampire from the lab.

MarkBaynard: Those sparkly vamps from TWILIGHT can't compete with these guys. They've drained enough of my blood to feed the entire Cullen clan.

MarkBaynard: I tried hanging a string of garlic on my IV pole but it turns out one of them is a big fan of Italian food. He took the garlic AND my blood.

MarkBaynard: If you'll excuse me, I have to go surrender my veins (and what's left of my soul) to Count Crapula.

MarkBaynard: Hopefully my suffering will give you cheer.

MarkBaynard: Goodnight Tweetheart...

Friday, June 17—1:15 A.M.

MarkBaynard: So how many days (and nights) do I have to talk to you without getting a reply before it qualifies as stalking?

MarkBaynard: At this point in my life even a visit from the police would qualify as a welcome diversion. (Or Chris Hansen from TO CATCH A PREDATOR.)

MarkBaynard: The one thing they don't tell you about dying (or trying not to die) is how freaking boring it can be.

MarkBaynard: If I had a hospital, I'd fix it up like Michael Jackson's Neverland with giraffes and carousels and roller coasters.

MarkBaynard: At least then I'd have a good reason to spend most of the day puking.

MarkBaynard: Or maybe it would be better to do it up like the Playboy Mansion with a lot of interchangeable blondes with interchangeable boobs.

MarkBaynard: At least then I'd have a good reason to spend most of the day in bed.

MarkBaynard: Don't you think I'd look better in a silk smoking jacket with a vacuous blonde on each arm than in this hospital gown?

MarkBaynard: Speaking of Michael Jackson, I entertained myself this morning by reading his autopsy report online.

MarkBaynard: Odd Thing to Read After an Autopsy: "He was in much better health than we expected." Well, yeah…except for the DEAD part.

MarkBaynard: Since I'm doing nothing, I have nothing to do but imagine what you're doing.

MarkBaynard: Besides sitting there waiting for Congress to come pry your incandescent lightbulbs out of your cold, dead hand, of course.

MarkBaynard: You're probably busy tweeting with some other English lit prof on sabbatical who doesn't have lymphoma and has actually been to Paris.

MarkBaynard: I hope it was only a one-frappucino day for you. I hope the words flowed from your fingertips like rivers of dark chocolate.

MarkBaynard: I hope Buffy the Mouse Slayer didn't eat Willow Tum-Tum. Or you.

MarkBaynard: I hope you're going to forgive me someday.

MarkBaynard: Goodnight Tweetheart…

Sunday, June 18—3:31 A.M.

MarkBaynard: Hey, babe. (Do I sound too much like Tommy Lee talking to Pam Anderson in one of those sex tapes?)

MarkBaynard: It's 3:30 a.m. and it feels like even the angels are sleeping.

MarkBaynard: The veil between their world and ours gets really thin at this time of the morning.

MarkBaynard: The hospital feels just like that one in HALLOWEEN 2 with the badly lit corridors & deserted nursing stations.

MarkBaynard: I keep expecting Michael Myers to pop by and offer to carve a jack-o'-lantern out of my brain.

MarkBaynard: I've had a couple of really sucky days. The doctor prescribed some new mondo pain meds so now I'm in pain AND high as the proverbial kite.

MarkBaynard: I've always tried not to tweet you when I was drugged up because I was afraid you'd think I was a junkie.

MarkBaynard: But now that you KNOW I'm a junkie, what does it matter?

MarkBaynard: I wish this was one of those Nicholas Sparks movies where everybody dies w/ great hair & a romantic theme song.

MarkBaynard: He always leaves out the puking. And the whining.

MarkBaynard: If I had a theme song it would probably be "B-Boys Makin' with the Freak Freak" by the Beastie Boys.

MarkBaynard: I'd say I wish I was dead right now, but it would be kind of redundant.

MarkBaynard: I'd say I wish you were here, but I don't wish anybody was stuck in this hellhole with me, not even my worst enemy.

MarkBaynard: Not even the neckless jock who stole my lunch money (and my briefcase) and stuffed me in my own locker in the 7th grade.

MarkBaynard: Okay...maybe him.

MarkBaynard: I dreamed about my son last night.

MarkBaynard: It was so wonderful to see him, but he was standing at the end of a long tunnel and no matter how fast or hard I ran, I couldn't reach him.

MarkBaynard: I guess we don't need Freud to interpret that one, do we?

MarkBaynard: I wish I had dreamed about you too.

MarkBaynard: zo, odd upi dp, ivj zoy hryd dp ;pmr;u yjod yo,r pg mohjy/

MarkBaynard: Oops…sorry. Had my fingers on the wrong keys. Can't remember what I was going to say anyway. Something deeply profound, I'm sure.

MarkBaynard: I never knew I could miss your voice so much when I've never even heard it.

MarkBaynard: Goodnight Twe

It was just as well that Mark's tweets ended there because the screen of the laptop was swimming before Abby's eyes. She groped blindly for the hem of her T-shirt, using it to scrub at her tear-stained face until her desk calendar came into focus.

Mark's last unfinished tweet had been posted over forty-eight hours ago. She sat there in the dark for a long time, bathed in the glow from the laptop screen. Reading Mark's tweets had been like tearing the scab off a wound just as it was beginning to heal.

She minimized Twitter and opened her Tweetdeck. Her hand hovered over the mouse. With one click of her fingertip she could Unfollow or even Block him. She could go back to living her safe little life in her safe little sublet apartment with no drama or needless complications other than the ones she created herself between the pages of her novels. She could look back on the bond they'd forged as nothing but a silly diversion. Something to distract her from the mundane, and often achingly lonely, reality of life as a single woman in New York City.

Like a disembodied appendage from some old sixties horror movie, her hand slowly drifted away from the mouse and toward the keyboard of the laptop. After a brief hesitation, her fingers attacked the keys, pounding out four words: *What are you wearing?*

She hit the Return key with a decisive click of her pinkie, then sat back in her chair and waited.

And waited some more.

As the digital clock in the corner of her screen ticked away the minutes, she struggled to convince herself that Mark was just fine. He was probably watching *Home Improvement* reruns on TV Land or sleeping off the effects of too much pain medication. As time dragged on, her pulse began to hammer in her ears, making her feel a little sick herself.

She closed her eyes, no longer able to bear the sight of the brightly lit Tweetdeck. What if something was wrong? *Really* wrong? What if she'd wasted too much time being pissed off at him?

What if the profound thing Mark had been trying to say when he'd ended up with his fingers on the wrong letters of the keyboard was good-bye? What if—

Her eyes flew open as the computer chirped, announcing the arrival of a new tweet.

Chapter Fourteen

Tuesday, June 21—7:45 P.M.

Abby_Donovan: What are you wearing?

MarkBaynard: Hospital gown flapping open in the back. Clear IV tubing. Look of bitter resignation. You?

Abby_Donovan: Coffee-stained sweats, Carrie White's prom queen crown from CARRIE, and a bucket of blood.

MarkBaynard: Oh hell...you're gonna kick my ass, aren't you?

Abby_Donovan: Let's put it this way. If you didn't wish you were dead before, you will by the time I'm through with you.

MarkBaynard: I'm guessing you're about to break out that whip-wielding dominatrix costume because I have been a Very Bad Boy.

Abby_Donovan: I'm polishing my handcuffs even as we speak.

MarkBaynard: Have I ever told you how cute you are when you're mad?

Abby_Donovan: Have I ever told you I have your mother on my speed dial?

MarkBaynard: And they say death and public speaking are man's two greatest fears!

Abby_Donovan: Before we even have this conversation, I'd like to know what other fibs you've told.

MarkBaynard: Well, I'm not really crazy about Insane Clown Posse. I've always preferred Anthrax or Slayer.

Abby_Donovan: Are you even divorced or was that a lie too?

MarkBaynard: I'm so divorced my ex-wife is engaged to another man.

Abby_Donovan: She didn't waste much time, did she?

MarkBaynard: He was already warming up in the bullpen before she left me.

Abby_Donovan: She cheated?

MarkBaynard: I can't really blame her. She was looking for something different in a guy. Like a potential survival rate higher than 20%.

Abby_Donovan: She cheated AFTER you got sick? Was she in the bathroom during the "in sickness and in health" segment of your wedding ceremony?

MarkBaynard: That's what I get for letting her talk me into writing our own vows.

Abby_Donovan: Let me guess. She called you her soul mate and promised to cleave to you until death did you part...or at least until she got a better offer.

MarkBaynard: There was something about rainbows & candles & maybe even ponies. But nothing about chemo or holding the trash can for me while I puked.

Abby_Donovan: And we thought WE had intimacy issues!

MarkBaynard: I've missed you. A guy can only talk to his life-size cardboard cutout of Hillary Clinton for so long before she starts to talk back.

Abby_Donovan: Please tell me they didn't let you bring that thing to the hospital?

MarkBaynard: What can I say? She squeaks less than my inflatable doll.

Abby_Donovan: I was hoping you were stuck watching a WIFE SWAP marathon on Lifetime.

MarkBaynard: Actually I've been watching PLANET EARTH—the best video Valium invented since the Teletubbies. So soothing!

Abby_Donovan: Yeah, at least until the baby elephant wanders off into the desert to die and the chimps start ripping off each other's faces.

MarkBaynard: Oh gee, thanks a lot! Spoil the ending for me, why don't you?

Abby_Donovan: Wait until I tell you what happens to Old Yeller.

MarkBaynard: Isn't it bad enough that I had to learn what happened to Beth in LITTLE WOMEN from an episode of FRIENDS?

Abby_Donovan: I figured you'd be watching SEX, LIES & VIDEOTAPE or maybe Jim Carrey in LIAR, LIAR.

MarkBaynard: Just so you know...I lied about my career too. I'm really an underwear model for Calvin Klein.

Abby_Donovan: That's odd, because just yesterday I found a pic of some guy named Mark Baynard on the faculty page of the Ole Miss website.

MarkBaynard: You naughty little vixen! We had a bargain! No peeking!

Abby_Donovan: At least you weren't lying about the houndstooth jacket with the leather patches on the elbows.

MarkBaynard: It was a gift from Calvin Klein.

Abby_Donovan: And just for the record, you look more like Seth Rogen than Hugh Jackman.

MarkBaynard: There's-Just-More-Of-Me-To-Love Seth Rogen? Or Slimmed-Down-For-The-Role-Of-Green-Hornet Seth Rogen?

Abby_Donovan: In-Between-You're-So-Cuddly-I-Kinda-Wanna-Have-Your-Baby Seth Rogen. You have beautiful hair (she added sulkily).

MarkBaynard: I did.

Abby_Donovan: Well, I always did like the new Andre Agassi look.

MarkBaynard: Thanks to the chemo and these damn steroids, I'm rocking more of a Homer Simpson/Dr. Evil look these days.

Abby_Donovan: Dr. Evil is WAY sexier than Austin Powers.

MarkBaynard: Very few women can resist a man with a volcano lair. Or a hairless cat named Mr. Bigglesworth.

Abby_Donovan: I'm not going to let you shave Willow Tum-Tum just so you can impress girls. Maybe Buffy, though.

MarkBaynard: Before you decide if you want to be one of those girls, there's one more thing you should know.

Abby_Donovan: You're really a Lancome-wearing, Cher-impersonating drag queen, aren't you? (Not that there's anything wrong with that.)

MarkBaynard: I wish it was that simple. While

we were...on our break...I kind of...sort of...um... read your first novel. (I duck...I run.)

Abby_Donovan: Who's the naughty little vixen now?

MarkBaynard: What can I say? I thought it was time to replace Hillary with the photo of you on the back of the book.

Abby_Donovan: Please tell me you didn't glue my face over hers.

MarkBaynard: Let's put it this way. You look really hot in a severe charcoal gray pantsuit.

Abby_Donovan: Well...what did you think?

MarkBaynard: About the novel or the photo?

Abby_Donovan: How shallow do you think I am? The photo, of course.

MarkBaynard: If Angelina and Jen had a love child, it would be you.

Abby_Donovan: That's so much better than Marge Simpson and Marilyn Manson. What about the novel? Did you like it as well as the photo?

MarkBaynard: I think the critics who called it the Next Great American Novel were wrong.

MarkBaynard: Abby? Are you still there? Did you hang up on me again?

Abby_Donovan: I should have expected as much from a tight-assed English lit professor who thinks HE's going to write the Great American Novel.

MarkBaynard: Your book wasn't the Next Great American Novel. It was the 2nd Greatest American Novel. Your new book will be the greatest.

Abby_Donovan: Forget I mentioned that whole "tight-assed" part, okay?

MarkBaynard: Does this mean I'm forgiven?

Abby_Donovan: Nope. It just means I'm going to stick around and keep kicking your ass until you get out of that hospital and I can kick it in person.

MarkBaynard: I love it when you talk dirty.

Abby_Donovan: Goodnight Niles

MarkBaynard: Goodnight Daphne

Abby_Donovan: Goodnight Frasier

MarkBaynard: Goodnight Roz

Abby_Donovan: Goodnight Bulldog

MarkBaynard: Goodnight Maris

Abby_Donovan: Goodnight Marty

MarkBaynard: Goodnight Tweetheart...

Thursday, June 22—4:15 P.M.

MarkBaynard: What are you wearing?

Abby_Donovan: My naughty nurse costume. http://tweetpic.com/2825190617

MarkBaynard: I'd tell you what I'm wearing,

but I think my heart just stopped. I can hear Nurse Ratched coming down the hall with the crash cart.

Abby_Donovan: All I can hear is my new neighbor's 3-year-old riding up and down the hall-way outside my apartment on his tricycle.

MarkBaynard: Have you tried telling him you have a big oven where you bake unruly children?

Abby_Donovan: I'm preheating it even as we speak.

MarkBaynard: So how is the writing going?

Abby_Donovan: VIEW FROM MY LAPTOP: http://tweetpic.com/2825190618.

MarkBaynard: Whoa! Chapter Fourteen al-ready? I guess I know what you were using all your words for when you weren't wasting them on wishing me dead.

Abby_Donovan: I think I might actually finish the book before the end of July. Loathing you was extremely conducive to my creativity.

MarkBaynard: Then I shall consider myself an inspiration to women everywhere.

Abby_Donovan: Are you alone right now?

MarkBaynard: Not anymore.

Abby_Donovan: You know what I mean. Is anybody there with you?

MarkBaynard: I thought I heard my mom's flying monkeys circling earlier, but it was just the med-ivac helicopter delivering a piping fresh kidney.

Abby_Donovan: You've never mentioned your dad.

MarkBaynard: He has a used Chevy business to run so he can keep my mom in booze & cigarettes. Virginia Slims Lights don't come cheap these days.

Abby_Donovan: What about your little sister? You said she adored you.

MarkBaynard: And I adore her back. Which is exactly why I'm not asking her to put her life on hold so she can watch me foolishly cling to mine.

Abby_Donovan: And your little boy?

Abby_Donovan: Mark, did I stick my big ole size 8 1/2 foot in my mouth?

MarkBaynard: I never lied to you about my son. I haven't seen him in over 6 months.

Abby_Donovan: Because of your treatment?

MarkBaynard: Because his mom could afford a better lawyer than me. She believes he's still young enough to forget me if things don't...work out...

Abby_Donovan: That's the most awful thing I've ever heard.

MarkBaynard: No, the most awful thing was when I called to try to talk to him and heard him in the background calling her new boyfriend "Daddy."

Abby_Donovan: Oh God. How can you let her get away with that?

MarkBaynard: Don't have the strength right now to fight her & this damn disease. I have to choose my battles so I can live to fight for him another day.

Abby_Donovan: She's wrong, you know. He won't forget you.

MarkBaynard: Of course he won't. His daddy makes the best grilled cheese and bacon sandwiches on the planet...

MarkBaynard: Plus his mom hates for him to have any kind of sugar so I used to sneak him Little Debbie Oatmeal Creme Pies when she wasn't looking.

Abby_Donovan: THINGS YOU WISH YOU'D SAID TO YOUR EX: "Everybody told me I was too good for you. They were right."

MarkBaynard: THINGS YOU WISH YOU'D SAID TO YOUR EX: "Yes, dear, those pants DO make your ass look fat."

Abby_Donovan: THINGS YOU WISH YOU'D SAID TO YOUR EX: "Oops, I was wrong. Size really DOES matter."

MarkBaynard: THINGS YOU WISH YOU'D SAID TO YOUR EX: "It's not me. It really IS you."

Abby_Donovan: So where in the world is Mark Baynard today?

MarkBaynard: I'd have to relinquish my honorary International Man of Mystery status if I told you my GPS coordinates.

Abby_Donovan: Not if you kill me after you tell me. So what time is it there?

MarkBaynard: Time for you to stop trying to trick me into revealing my whereabouts by telling you what time zone I'm in.

Abby_Donovan: Curses! Foiled again! I had at least hoped to narrow it down to the North American Continent. Or Zimbabwe.

MarkBaynard: Too bad I'm on to you and your nefarious ways. I'm trained to resist all forms of torture meted out by you and your little henchkitties.

Abby_Donovan: You haven't seen what Buffy the Mouse Slayer can do with some catnip and a cattle prod. Why won't you tell me where you are?

MarkBaynard: So you can send me some flowers? Or maybe one of those musical Hallmark cards that plays "I Will Survive"?

Abby_Donovan: I was thinking more along the lines of something by Death Cab for Cutie.

MarkBaynard: No thank you. You can keep your

flowers and your cards. I'd much rather have you loathe me than pity me.

Abby_Donovan: Congratulations. It's working.

MarkBaynard: I think that's one of the real reasons my wife left. After I relapsed she decided she pitied me more than she had ever loved me.

Abby_Donovan: Do you still love her?

MarkBaynard: At the moment I can't even work up the energy to hate her. Although I hate what she's doing to me and to our son.

Abby_Donovan: What was it you told me on our last "date"? "Loathing is a form of passion. It's apathy that kills a relationship."

MarkBaynard: Exactly. They say that living well is the best revenge. At this point in our relationship, I'd settle for just living.

Abby_Donovan: How long do you have before your big treatment?

MarkBaynard: A week. Maybe two. It depends on how many viable stem cells they were able to harvest.

Abby_Donovan: You said this procedure was experimental. Just how dangerous is it?

MarkBaynard: Somewhere between pissing off Sharon Stone in BASIC INSTINCT and shouting "Jesus loves you" in a crowded mosque.

Abby_Donovan: Will it be painful?

MarkBaynard: Only if I survive.

Abby_Donovan: I'd probably be curled into a fetal position if I were you. I don't see how you can be so flip about the whole thing.

MarkBaynard: You know what they say. It's better to laugh than to cry. Or to gibber in terror.

Abby_Donovan: Did you learn that from Yoda?

MarkBaynard: No…from Guitar Hero, my true Zen master. The only way to get through this life is to hit as many notes as you can and try not to die.

Abby_Donovan: Would you mind trying really, REALLY hard?

MarkBaynard: Only for you. I have to go now. I think I hear those flying monkeys headed back this way.

Abby_Donovan: Don't tell them where to find me.

MarkBaynard: "I'll get you, my pretty! And your little cats too!"

Abby_Donovan: Goodnight Principal Belding

MarkBaynard: Goodnight Jessie

Abby_Donovan: Goodnight Zach

MarkBaynard: Goodnight Lisa

Abby_Donovan: Goodnight Slater

MarkBaynard: Goodnight Kelly

Abby_Donovan: Goodnight Screech

MarkBaynard: Goodnight Tweetheart…

Sunday, June 26—10:45 P.M.

Abby_Donovan: What are you wearing?

Abby_Donovan: Mark? I haven't heard from you in a couple of days and it's starting to worry me. And Willow Tum-Tum.

Abby_Donovan: If you're just playing hard to get, it's working. Another day of this and you'll have me on my knees shamelessly begging for your tweets.

Abby_Donovan: I hope you're okay. I hope the flying monkeys and lab vamps didn't join forces to defeat you.

Abby_Donovan: I hope you slept like a baby last night and didn't dream of a single Kardashian.

Abby_Donovan: I hope you'll tweet me as soon as you're able. I'm scared.

Monday, June 27—2:37 A.M.

MarkBaynard: What are you wearing?

Abby_Donovan: Coffee-stained sweats and Doris Day's pillbox hat from…well…just about any of her movies. You?

MarkBaynard: I twisted my bedsheet into Bluto's toga from ANIMAL HOUSE. I didn't really think you'd be up. It's 2:30 in the morning in New York.

Abby_Donovan: I couldn't sleep.

MarkBaynard: Isn't that my line?

Abby_Donovan: Maybe insomnia is contagious. Where have you been?

MarkBaynard: I had to take a brief tour of the cardiac care unit. I'm thinking of investing in a time share.

Abby_Donovan: Are you okay? What happened?

MarkBaynard: They forced me to watch a really boring video starring a lot of happy old people playing golf just to get the free gift.

Abby_Donovan: Have I ever told you I don't have much of a sense of humor at 2:30 in the morning?

MarkBaynard: It was nothing major. Just a little blip on the heart monitor. Some of the drugs can damage your muscles. Including the muscle of love.

Abby_Donovan: Um...Mark...I think "muscle of love" refers to an entirely different part of the anatomy.

MarkBaynard: Oh...well, in that case, the drugs I'm on can QUADRUPLE the size of your muscles.

Abby_Donovan: No wonder you're so popular with the naughty nurses. Will this setback interfere with your procedure?

MarkBaynard: No. Now that my heart is beating again, everything is a go.

Abby_Donovan: Your heart stopped???!!!

MarkBaynard: Just for a few seconds. Some guy in a bathrobe tried to drag me kicking & screaming into the white light, but I told him to go to hell.

Abby_Donovan: Did they have to shock you?

MarkBaynard: Just a little. All it took was showing me Lady Gaga's new video.

Abby_Donovan: I was getting really worried about you.

MarkBaynard: I tried to bribe the CCU nurse into giving me my laptop, but all I had to offer her was the leftover lime Jell-O from my lunch tray.

Abby_Donovan: You should have offered her your tapioca pudding. I've heard it works every time.

MarkBaynard: Enough about my adventures. What have you been up to?

Abby_Donovan: Well, I went over to the Bronx to visit my mom in the nursing home this afternoon.

MarkBaynard: How was she?

Abby_Donovan: Not bad. Elvis was dropping by later and that always puts her in a good mood.

MarkBaynard: Was he bringing Napoleon and Teddy Roosevelt with him?

Abby_Donovan: No...just Janis Joplin and Jim Morrison.

MarkBaynard: If I'd have gone into the light with that guy in the bathrobe, I could have dropped by too.

Abby_Donovan: Sometimes when your mom is demented she says hilariously inappropriate things that make you want to gouge out your eyes with a fork.

MarkBaynard: My mom does that too. But I'd have to use a spork, since that's all they give you here.

Abby_Donovan: I think my mom would like you.

MarkBaynard: Because we're both demented? Your mom is lucky to have you. You're a good girl, Abby Donovan.

Abby_Donovan: A good little Catholic schoolgirl? I thought I was a naughty little vixen?

MarkBaynard: Only on Tuesdays and Thursdays. Why don't you go get some sleep? I'm still a little wrung out myself.

Abby_Donovan: Thank you for letting me know you're okay.

MarkBaynard: I'm always okay when you're around.

Abby_Donovan: Goodnight Potsie

MarkBaynard: Goodnight Mrs. C.

Abby_Donovan: Goodnight Richie

MarkBaynard: Goodnight Joanie

Abby_Donovan: Goodnight Arnold

MarkBaynard: Goodnight Pinkie

Abby_Donovan: Goodnight Arthur

MarkBaynard: Goodnight Tweetheart...

Wednesday, June 29—9:58 P.M.

MarkBaynard: What are you wearing?

Abby_Donovan: A purple Sue Sylvester track suit with approximately 2 lbs of Buffy hair on it. You?

MarkBaynard: A really pissed-off expression and what feels like 35 yards of IV tubing I'm about to use to hang myself. Or someone else.

Abby_Donovan: Bad day?

MarkBaynard: I'm this close to throwing a hydrotherapy unit through the window and making my escape.

Abby_Donovan: Where would you go?

MarkBaynard: Florence? The Loire Valley? Tuscany? Maybe Rome?...

MarkBaynard: We could drink too much wine, dance naked in the fountains & make mad, passionate love until dawn.

Abby_Donovan: Or until the polizia come to lock us up.

MarkBaynard: Trust me. An Italian jail cell would be preferable to this place.

Abby_Donovan: Only if some big, hairy Sicilian doesn't make you his bitch.

MarkBaynard: I think you just described my night nurse. And I'm already her bitch.

Abby_Donovan: You're not losing your sense of humor, are you? I've always heard it was the last thing to go.

MarkBaynard: You know what they say—dying is easy; comedy is hard.

Abby_Donovan: Are you still hitting as many notes as you can?

MarkBaynard: God knows I'm trying. If I were God, I'd be zapping people w/lightning bolts on an hourly basis. Forgot to use a turn signal? ZAP!!!

Abby_Donovan: Didn't wipe off frappucino cup before handing it to me? ZAP!!!

MarkBaynard: Take 20 minutes to sing the National Anthem before a ball game? ZAP!!!

Abby_Donovan: Charge me $8.50 for a small popcorn at the movies? ZAP!!!

MarkBaynard: Too busy worrying about finishing up your shift to give me my next dose of pain meds. ZAP!!!

Abby_Donovan: If you'll tell me where you are, I'll come do my Shirley MacLaine impression from TERMS OF ENDEARMENT. I'll get you those meds.

MarkBaynard: If you were Shirley MacLaine, your psychic friends could tell you where I was.

Abby_Donovan: I think you're getting Shirley mixed up with Dionne Warwick. Shirley's the one who was Charlemagne's lover in her past life.

MarkBaynard: I must have been Genghis Freaking Khan in my past life. That's the only thing that would explain the day I've had.

Abby_Donovan: What can I do?

MarkBaynard: Could you just talk to me for a minute? I'm having trouble concentrating on anything but the sound of your voice.

Abby_Donovan: You think YOU'VE had a bad day? If you want to really look death in the face, you should try trimming Buffy the Mouse Slayer's claws.

Abby_Donovan: I only managed to get two of them done before being forced to call an exorcist.

Abby_Donovan: Even as a kitten, Buffy had the

look of a burgeoning serial killer. http://tweetpic .com/2825190620

Abby_Donovan: Today a stray cat tried to flag me down in the park as if to say "Take me home." Are Buffy & Willow signaling the mothership while I sleep?

Abby_Donovan: My day only got better when I found a scathing one-star review of my book on Amazon.

Abby_Donovan: I'd take these amateur reviewers more seriously if they'd say, "This book doesn't work for me"...

Abby_Donovan:...as opposed to "No more innocent trees should die in the service of this demon author."

Abby_Donovan: Tonight I watched some chick on the Food Channel make lobster tacos with chocolate-covered bacon in them.

Abby_Donovan: I know it sounds icky but it was DARK chocolate and APPLEWOOD bacon. That makes it okay, doesn't it? Wonder if she's married?

Abby_Donovan: Mark?

Abby_Donovan: Mark? Are you asleep?

Abby_Donovan: Sweet dreams, Tweetheart...

Tuesday, July 5—8:35 A.M.

MarkBaynard: What are you wearing?

Abby_Donovan: Coffee-stained sweats and Bill Murray's Proton Pack from GHOSTBUSTERS. You?

MarkBaynard: Coffee-stained sweats & a mortified blush...

MarkBaynard: Sorry I fell asleep on you the other night. My wife used to hate when I did that. Especially if she was on the bottom.

Abby_Donovan: It's probably not the first time someone has lapsed into a coma while reading my work. But they usually have to buy my book first.

MarkBaynard: I dreamed about a cat with Ted Bundy eyes spewing green pea soup and woke up with a terrible craving for dark chocolate and bacon.

Abby_Donovan: How is the pain today?

MarkBaynard: Somewhere between an ingrown toenail & hitting oneself repeatedly in the groin with a hammer.

Abby_Donovan: Have you had your meds?

MarkBaynard: Not yet. I wanted to stay coherent enough to let you know that you might not hear from me for a little while.

Abby_Donovan: Planning another tour of the cardiac care unit?

MarkBaynard: Dr. Horrible just came in to tell me I'll be in strict isolation for most of the next week. They've finally scheduled my procedure.

MarkBaynard: Abby?

Abby_Donovan: Tell me where you are. I'll come. Anywhere.

MarkBaynard: I'm afraid I can't let you do that. I've retreated to my volcano lair. No girls allowed.

Abby_Donovan: Mark, I was being serious.

MarkBaynard: So was I.

Abby_Donovan: Now you're really scaring me.

MarkBaynard: I kind of hate you, you know. Just a little bit.

Abby_Donovan: Why?

MarkBaynard: Before I met you I didn't have a whole hell of a lot to live for. My wife had left me. My son was gone...

MarkBaynard: I could laugh in the face of Death without worrying that he was going to kick my teeth in with his steel-toed boots.

Abby_Donovan: Tell me where you are. I'll bring my Proton Pack so we can fight him together. He can't be any tougher than the Stay Puft Marshmallow Man.

MarkBaynard: I'm afraid we'd cross our streams and he'd annihilate us both.

Abby_Donovan: It's a chance I'm willing to take.

MarkBaynard: But not one I'm willing to give you.

Abby_Donovan: I forgave you for lying to me. But I'll never forgive you if you die. I'll find your grave & let Buffy use it for a litter box.

MarkBaynard: Thank you for making me laugh. Thank you for making me forget...

MarkBaynard: And most of all, thank you for making me remember that there are still things in this world worth laughing about.

Abby_Donovan: Don't you tell me good-bye, Mark Baynard. Don't you dare tell me good-bye!

MarkBaynard: I'm not going to say good-bye. Or even "Until we tweet again." I'm just going to say...

MarkBaynard: Goodnight Tweetheart...

And just like that, he was gone.

Abby leaned back in her desk chair, her fingers frozen over the keyboard. She lifted her gaze to the window, but the world outside seemed no more substantial than a picture on a TV screen.

She knew deep in her heart that there would be

no point in pleading with Mark. No point in sending repeated tweets trying to coax him into relenting. His mind was made up. He was determined to march into this last battle all alone with nothing but his fragile hope for a shield.

Leaving her with nothing to do...but wait.

Chapter Fifteen

Abby blew through the doorway of the AT&T store, propelled by a violent gust of wind and rain. Even though there was no bear chasing her, she'd run nearly the entire half a mile between her apartment and the store. She doubled over and sucked in a few tortured gasps of air before straightening to take stock of her surroundings.

Several people in the crowded store were eyeing her with open suspicion. She wasn't sure she could blame them. She probably looked like something even the cat would decline to drag in.

She'd rushed out of the apartment without bothering to snag the elegant Burberry raincoat hanging in the back of her closet. She'd been too distracted to realize it was pouring down rain until she was halfway across Grand Army Plaza. By then she was already soaked to the skin so there hadn't seemed to be much point in going back for the raincoat.

She shook the soaking strands of her hair out of her eyes, accidentally spattering the shoppers closest to her. Ignoring their annoyed looks, she worked her way clumsily through their ranks until she reached the sales counter on the far side of the room, her faded Chuck Taylors squelching with each step.

A skinny white kid with acne scars, Harry Potter glasses, and a lopsided blond Afro was demonstrating the delights of the latest iPhone to a rapt couple who had *not* forgotten their Burberry raincoats when they left their swank Upper West Side apartment.

"Excuse me," Abby blurted out, wondering if she looked as wild-eyed as she felt. "I need a Crack-Berry...I mean a BlackBerry, or an iPhone!"

The clerk didn't even bother to glance at her. "If you'll take a number, ma'am, the next available associate will be with you as soon as possible."

Abby looked frantically around until she spotted the number dispenser at the end of the counter. The saucy little tongue of paper protruding from the mouth of the bright orange box was currently showing "467." The digital number on the screen over the counter read "433."

She inched sideways, struggling to place herself

in the clerk's line of sight and earning a justifiably irritated look from the couple.

"You don't understand," she said. "I haven't been able to leave my apartment in over four days because I'm expecting a message. A very *important* message."

"From your home planet?" the clerk ventured, slanting her hair a disparaging look. The wetter it got, the weirder it got. Abby could feel it coiling around her head like broken bedsprings as it soaked up every last drop of humidity in the air.

She sighed. The rational thing to do would be to take a number, take a seat, and patiently wait for the next available associate to help her.

She couldn't stay in her apartment forever. She'd already missed her regular Monday visit to her mother's nursing home and she and her agent were supposed to have lunch tomorrow to discuss a potential offer for her book from a small but very prestigious literary publisher. She could carry her laptop with her when she went out, but what if there was no WiFi connection available at her destination? And what about the time it took to travel from her apartment to wherever she was going? Mark could be tweeting her at that very moment while she stood there in a rapidly spreading puddle of rainwater, fighting the urge to grab the smug clerk by his skinny tie and yank him across the counter.

"Please," she whispered, feeling the humiliating sting of tears at the backs of her eyes. "I *really* need a new phone. It's a matter of life and death."

There must have been some hint of her anguish in her voice because for a fraction of a second, the young clerk looked at her and saw her. *Really* saw her in a way that New Yorkers rarely did.

Heaving a defeated sigh, he fished a brochure out from under the counter and handed it to the couple. "Why don't you guys check out the specs on our upcoming 5GS plan while you're waiting?"

They spared Abby a resentful pout, but dutifully huddled over the brochure together while the clerk entered Abby's current cell phone number into his computer terminal and consulted his monitor. "Your current contract won't be fulfilled until November, which means we can't offer you any discount whatsoever on a new phone. You'll have to pay the full retail price, which is five hundred and fifty—"

"I'll take it."

The clerk blinked owlishly at the platinum American Express card that had magically appeared in her hand. "O-o-o-okey-dokey," he sang out, plucking the card from her hand.

"One more thing?" Now that she was on the verge of having a brand-new phone in her hot little hands, Abby even managed to dredge up a grateful smile.

He paused before swiping the card, eyeing her warily. "Yes?"

"Could you show me how to download Tweet-deck?"

Abby gazed down at the sleek iPhone cradled in her palm, silently willing the haughty thing to do something—anything at all—that might acknowl-edge her existence. For all the good it had done her in the past three days, she might as well go ahead and hurl it into the Lake. With her luck, it would probably hit one of the boaters taking a leisurely row around the shoreline of Central Park's most fa-mous body of water.

Still gripping the phone as if it were some ancient talisman designed to ward off evil, she leaned back on the park bench and tilted her face to the sky. It was one of those perfect summer days when humidity fell and hope soared. Cotton puff clouds drifted across a crisp blue sky. The park was an oasis of green in the middle of the soaring gray canyons of the city, irresistibly drawing anyone starved for a breath of fresh air and the illusion of freedom.

Based on outward appearances, Abby's luck seemed to be changing. Her book was only a handful of chapters away from being done and she thought it was good, maybe even better than her first book. At that very minute her agent was hammering out the details of a nice six-figure deal with a starry-eyed editor eager to work with her on her next three projects. Abby might have to give up her Plaza sublet, but she would be able to keep Buffy and Willow Tum-Tum in kibble.

She was tired of living in a renovated hotel room anyway. The fragility of Mark's life had made her realize just how *impermanent* she had allowed her own life to become.

She had fooled herself into believing she was living the life she'd always dreamed of living when all she had been doing was hiding from it. But Mark had refused to let her hide. He had dragged her kicking and screaming through the streets of Paris, into the Tuscan sunshine, and past the fountains of Florence until she had finally found herself standing at the very peak of Blarney Castle with the rest of her life spread out below her. He had shown her what it really meant to live until you die, even if the countries you visited only existed in your imagination.

She didn't want to waste another minute sleeping

on a futon and living in someone else's apartment. She wanted a place to call her own—maybe a modest cottage in the Hamptons or some old Victorian house along the Jersey Shore that would require both elbow grease and love to become a home. A place where she could get three times the square footage for a mortgage that was half what she'd been paying in rent. She'd even considered returning to North Carolina, settling in Asheville or one of the other communities that welcomed artists with open arms.

Or she could simply spend the rest of her life sitting on this park bench, waiting for a tweet that might never come.

The clouds blurred before her eyes as she was forced to face the truth she'd been denying for the past week. She might never find out what had happened to Mark. Might never hear his voice again— a voice that had come to echo in her head as clearly as her own.

She blinked, bringing the clouds back into sharp focus.

She couldn't bring herself to assume the worst. Not yet. Mark might still be in strict isolation or struggling with the regimen of drugs they were giving him to prepare him for his treatment. Maybe he hadn't been able to use his leftover lime Jell-O to bribe Nurse Ratched into giving him his laptop.

He had been willing to hold on to hope even when it looked like all hope was lost. She owed him no less.

Tucking the phone in the pocket of her cargo shorts, she rose and headed for her apartment, where she could spend the rest of the afternoon eating Ben & Jerry's directly out of the container and gazing morosely at her laptop.

Her pocket chirped.

For a minute she thought her own heart was going to stop.

Fumbling to fish the phone out of the deep pocket of the baggy shorts, she raced toward a shady spot under the sheltering boughs of an oak where she would be able to read the display more clearly.

She swiped her finger frantically over the phone's touch screen until the Direct Message column of her mobile Tweetdeck appeared. The incoming tweet was accompanied by Mark's profile pic: a pensive John Cusack holding a boom box over his head as if his arms would never grow tired as long as there was still a chance of being heard by the girl he loved.

Abby felt a grin start to curve her lips, but it was replaced by a frown of confusion as she read the incoming tweet.

Thursday, July 14—1:22 P.M.

MarkBaynard: Are you Abby?

Abby_Donovan: I am.

MarkBaynard: Mark's Abby?

Abby_Donovan: I think so.

MarkBaynard: I'm Kate. Mark's little sister.

Abby_Donovan: Hi, Kate. I'm so glad to hear from you. How is he?

MarkBaynard: I'm on Facebook, but I have no clue what I'm doing when it comes to this Tweeter stuff.

Abby_Donovan: It's okay. I'm listening.

MarkBaynard: My brother will be going in for his treatment tomorrow and he left some instructions and a note for you.

Abby_Donovan: ???

MarkBaynard: Tell her Roger Daltrey can still kick David Cassidy's ass. Tell her she's prettier than Jen or Angelina. Tell her she was the love of my li

Abby_Donovan: Kate?

Abby_Donovan: Kate? Are you still there?

"Kate?" Abby whispered as the phone went dark and silent once again. "Mark?" she added in more of a breath than a whisper.

She slumped against the trunk of the tree, clutching the phone in fingers that had gone as numb as her heart. The sun was still filtering through the tender green leaves of the oak. The clouds were still drifting across the robin's-egg blue of the sky. Mothers were still chasing their laughing children and frolicking dogs around Bethesda Terrace. Lovers were still strolling hand in hand around the lake. Yet everything inside of Abby had gone quiet and still, as if she'd drawn in a breath she never expected to exhale.

"Damn you, Mark Baynard," she finally said in a voice she barely recognized as her own. "I won't let you do this." Shoving the phone back into the pocket of her shorts, she pushed herself away from the tree and took off for her apartment at a determined jog.

Chapter Sixteen

I'm sorry, ma'am. We're not at liberty to divulge that information."

As the hospital operator's tinny voice filled her ear, Abby winced. Since returning from the park several hours ago, she'd heard dozens of variations on the same theme and learned far more than she ever wanted to about the Health Insurance Portability and Accountability Act, or as it was known by the medically hip—HIPAA. Designed to protect a patient's medical information, the act's stringent privacy rule also made it nearly impossible to determine whether or not the individual in question actually existed or was simply a figment of your imagination.

In the eyes of the United States Department of Health and Human Services, asking a simple question like, "Can you tell me if Mark Baynard is—or was—a patient at your hospital?" was akin to requesting the nuclear codes for a Russian submarine.

"Still no luck?" Margo turned to ask Abby, shrugging her well-muscled shoulders to work the kinks out of them.

Responding to Abby's frantic distress signal, Margo had appeared on Abby's doorstep several hours ago, bearing a sack of warm donuts and a cardboard tray of emergency lattes. She'd spent the past several hours hunched over the desk, using Abby's laptop to Google the name and number of every hospital in the country that specialized in treating non-Hodgkins lymphoma, then narrowing down her finds to those with a reputation for conducting clinical trials. She would fill up a page with her notes, then pass them to where Abby sat curled up in a corner of the leather couch, the cordless phone pressed against her ear like an extra appendage.

A quick shake of Abby's head told Margo everything she needed to know.

While her friend returned to her search, Abby went down the most recent list Margo had given her, dialing one number after another until both her ear and her index finger went numb.

The very first call she'd made had been to Ole Miss. But Mark's employer hadn't been any more willing than the hospitals to reveal his current condition or whereabouts. Not even pretending to be one of his former besotted female students had softened their stony hearts.

Margo turned to hand her another sheet of paper, the worried look in her dark liquid eyes leaving little doubt that she believed Abby's desperate quest would end in heartbreak.

Abby snatched the paper from her friend's hand, avoiding those eyes. "Don't say it, Margo. Just keep Googling. I promise I'll have you back in Javier's bed in no time."

"It's not Javier. It's Guillermo," Margo informed her with a wounded flare of her regal nostrils. "And he has a photo shoot today so I won't be expecting him until late tonight."

"What's he going to be? Mr. October?"

"I'll have you know he's a perfectly respectable hand model."

"From what I saw of him, I never would have guessed his hands were his best feature."

"That's because you've never spent a night in his bed."

Smiling in spite of herself, Abby began to dial the next number on her list. The operator who answered sounded younger and kinder than most.

She actually heaved an apologetic sigh before proceeding to crush Abby's hopes. "I'm sorry, ma'am, but due to HIPAA regulations, we're not allowed to give out information on any of our patients."

Abby was about to hit the disconnect button and move on to the next number on the list when she realized exactly what the woman had said. She snatched the receiver back to her ear. "*Your* patients? Are you saying that Mark Baynard actually *is* your patient?"

There was an awkward moment of silence followed by a tentative swallow. "I'm afraid I wouldn't be allowed to divulge that information. Even if it was true."

"Thank you. Thank you so very much," Abby said softly before lowering the receiver.

She ran her trembling finger down Margo's elegant scrawl until she found the number she had just dialed. She traced it over to the right-hand column of the page—*New York-Presbyterian Hospital*.

Handling the loose leaf of notebook paper as if it were a scrap of Egyptian parchment in danger of crumbling to dust in her hands, Abby carried it over to the desk and laid it next to the laptop.

She pointed to the entry in question. "Can you pull this one up for me again?"

There must have been something in her voice that stopped Margo from offering either a question or a protest. She simply typed the name of the hospital in the Search box, her bronzed nails flying over the keyboard, then clicked on the first result that came up.

According to its sleek yet user-friendly website, the New York-Presbyterian Hospital on East Sixty-eighth Street was a state-of-the-art medical center. It was also home to the Treatment Center for Lymphoma and Myeloma. Abby leaned over Margo's shoulder to read the brochure-ready copy on the web page:

> *The Center pioneered the growth of radio-labeled antibody treatment for lymphoma, and has conducted a significant number of clinical trials in this area. The Center also was among the first to combine chemotherapy with radiolabeled antibodies as part of initial therapy for patients newly diagnosed with lymphoma. Several clinical trials are also under way to evaluate vaccines administered following chemotherapy to delay or prevent recurrence of tumor. The Center's B cell lymphoma program continues to attract patients from all over the world with its innovative immunological therapies.*

Still gazing blindly at the screen, Abby straightened.

New York-Presbyterian. East Sixty-eighth Street.

She didn't know whether to laugh or cry. All this time Mark had been less than ten short blocks from her apartment. A brisk walk on a sunny afternoon.

Feeling as if she were sleepwalking through a dream, she returned to the phone. Her hands were oddly steady as she dialed the number a second time. A different operator answered this time— one who sounded far more seasoned and far less likely to accidentally reveal confidential information.

Abby chose her words with care. "I know you're not allowed to give out any information on your patients, but would it be possible for you to page a member of a patient's family for me?"

"Name please?"

A shaky sigh escaped Abby as she silently prayed Mark's little sister wasn't married yet. "Kate Baynard."

"Please hold."

Abby swallowed hard, gripping the receiver for dear life. She could feel Margo standing behind her, her own breathing stilted.

The operator returned to the line, her tone as brisk and impersonal as a recording's. "Just one moment."

Then there was a click and a woman who sounded both very young and very tired said, "This is Kate. Can I help you?"

"This is Abby, Kate." As Margo squeezed her shoulder, Abby closed her eyes, finally allowing the tears to flow. "Mark's Abby."

Abby strode down a long beige corridor that could have belonged in any hospital anywhere in the country. She hadn't brought flowers or a musical Hallmark card that played "I Will Survive." She hadn't even taken the time to change out of her coffee-stained T-shirt and faded cargo shorts.

The warm hues of the brightly patterned carpet did their best to offset the chilly glow of the overhead fluorescents. Open doors flanked the hallway, but Abby kept her gaze fixed straight ahead, resisting her natural urge to steal a peek into each room as she passed. These patients had already lost so much. They at least deserved their privacy.

A number on the wall informed her that she had arrived at her destination. The door to the room was half ajar. The overhead light had been turned off, leaving the room bathed in the dim glow of a bedside lamp. Several of the other rooms had had canned laughter or muffled voices drifting out into the corridor from the flat-panel TVs mounted on the walls, but the only sound drifting out of this room was the rhythmic beep of a heart monitor.

Abby lifted her hand, but before she could knock she spotted the young woman curled up in the recliner just inside the door. She had made herself a cozy nest out of a hospital blanket and furnished it with a stack of Harlequin romances, the latest novel by Stieg Larsson, and a battered Dell laptop, which appeared to be in sleep mode just like its owner. The floor around the chair was littered with empty Styrofoam cups and several packages of half-eaten crackers that could have only come from a hospital vending machine.

With her curly brown hair caught back from her face in a banana clip and her freckled face scrubbed clean of makeup, Kate Baynard looked very young. The fact that she had drifted back into a deep doze when she had known Abby was coming revealed the depth of her exhaustion. It was clear she had no intention of leaving her brother's bedside as long as he might need her.

Abby carefully tucked the blanket around the girl's shoulders before turning to the bed.

There was no sign of Hillary Clinton, but a hardcover copy of *Time Out of Mind* by Abigail Donovan rested facedown on the bedside table.

Shaking her head ruefully, Abby studied the younger and glossier version of herself smiling up at her from the back of the dust jacket. She was surprised to realize she no longer either envied or pitied that woman. Maybe in time she might even grow to like her.

She turned to gaze down at the man in the bed, overwhelmed by a rush of tenderness. They were strangers in so many ways, but not in any ways that mattered.

He opened his eyes and blinked up at her. Then blinked again. His eyes widened with gratifying shock as he realized that live or die, he wasn't going to do it without her.

"Hello, Dr. Evil," she said softly. "Surely you didn't think you could elude me forever."

He smiled then, and it was a smile she would have known anywhere. It was the smile Sam had given Frodo at the end of *Return of the King*. The smile that said, "I will always be your friend. I will always love you no matter what you've done and no matter what you'll ever do."

It was *that* smile that lit up his eyes as he reached for her hand and said, "Hello, Tweetheart."

Epilogue

*M*arkBaynard: What are you wearing?

Abby_Donovan: A hopeful smile and the thigh-high black vinyl boots Julia Roberts wore in PRETTY WOMAN.

MarkBaynard: Is that all you're wearing? Because if it is, my smile just got a lot more hopeful.

Abby_Donovan: Don't get your hopes up too high, mister. This is only our third date and I don't put out until at least the dessert course of the fourth.

MarkBaynard: Don't all those romantic interludes over the congealed cottage cheese in the hospital cafeteria count for anything?

Abby_Donovan: Well, there was the night we shared the Diet Dr Pepper ice cream float and I almost let you get to first base.

MarkBaynard: And the time I stumbled over

my IV pole in the hallway and accidentally got to second base.

Abby_Donovan: Ha! I never believed that was an accident.

MarkBaynard: You and the grumpy old lady in room 337.

Abby_Donovan: So that's why she called hospital security!

MarkBaynard: No, that was because I flashed her after she stole the lime Jell-O off my tray.

Abby_Donovan: So what are YOU wearing?

MarkBaynard: Anything but a hospital gown.

Abby_Donovan: I've heard that's a very trendy look these days. Especially on the runway in Milan and among escaped mental patients.

MarkBaynard: Is Margo still trying to warn you not to go out with me?

Abby_Donovan: After playing Scrabble with you and Kate all those times in the hospital, she's even more convinced you're a serial killer.

MarkBaynard: She just hasn't forgiven me for insisting "oxyphenbutazone" was a word.

Abby_Donovan: She hasn't forgiven you because it WAS a word.

MarkBaynard: I got a profane text from her today challenging me to a game of "Words with Frenemies."

Abby_Donovan: When she found out where I was meeting you for our date this time, she accused you of trying to sweep me off my feet.

MarkBaynard: I've spent enough of our relationship off mine. Don't you think it's your turn?

Abby_Donovan: You know I would have been perfectly happy to meet you on the Poet's Walk in Central Park. Or the basement of Macy's.

MarkBaynard: I haven't seen you in almost a month. I wanted our third date to be something special.

Abby_Donovan: How did your visit with Mini-Mark go?

MarkBaynard: Except for his hair, he's more like a Mini–Joe Pesci right now. Threatened to put a mob hit out on his mom if she wouldn't let me see him.

Abby_Donovan: See . . . I told you he would never forget his daddy!

MarkBaynard: That's because I brought him a box of Oatmeal Creme Pies. As long as I keep a lifetime supply of Little Debbie's on hand, I'm gold.

Abby_Donovan: Did he like the pics of Buffy the Mouse Slayer and Willow Tum-Tum I e-mailed him?

MarkBaynard: His mom and stepdad will

never know another moment of peace until they get him a cat of his own. Which is an added bonus for me.

Abby_Donovan: I hope you know I wouldn't have blamed you if you had decided to stay in Mississippi.

MarkBaynard: I was sort of hoping it would break your heart.

Abby_Donovan: I said I wouldn't blame you. I didn't say it wouldn't break my heart.

MarkBaynard: It would have broken my doctor's heart if I had missed my follow-up appointment.

Abby_Donovan: You've already been? Why didn't you tell me? I thought you promised there'd be no more secrets between us!

MarkBaynard: And there won't be. I was going to keep our date no matter what news he gave me.

Abby_Donovan: (Deep breath.) So what did he say?

MarkBaynard: Turn around and I'll tell you.

Abby lowered her iPhone to the table and rose from her chair, slowly pivoting to find Mark strolling across the spacious plaza of the Place de L'Alma. Behind him the graceful latticework of the Eiffel Tower was silhouetted against a lavender sky. The sun had dipped below the horizon while Abby waited at the cafe for him. The deepening dusk only made the glow of the city lights reflecting off the inky waters of the Seine seem more luminous and magical.

Mark's gait was strong and steady, his body already recovering from most of the ravages of the chemo and steroids. He would never be Batman or Hugh Jackman, but somehow that made him even more beautiful and dear to her eyes. He didn't have to be larger than life. It was enough that he was alive.

She had curled up next to him in his hospital bed while they watched endless episodes of *The Golden Girls* and season one of *Veronica Mars*. She had held the trash can for him while he puked. Held his hand during those dark, endless nights when pain and the drugs they gave him to take the edge off that pain had driven him half out of his mind. Held on to hope even when his own had begun to flag.

Yet as he stopped in front of her, giving her a lopsided grin as he tucked his own cell phone in the pocket of his jacket, she felt her throat tighten with a peculiar shyness, almost as if it was their very first date.

Which, in many ways, it was.

Instead of thigh-high boots, she was wearing sensible flats, perfect for strolling the Paris streets arm in arm with the man she loved. She'd accessorized her simple black wool dress with one or two of the obligatory cat hairs that always ended up in her carry-on. Her sweater was the perfect weight to ward off the autumn chill of the mild November night.

There would be no more hiding behind the walls of her sublet apartment or the columns of her Tweetdeck or even the endless parade of doctors and nurses at the hospital. There was just the two of them and the bottle of wine chilling on the table behind her.

Finding it easier in that moment to touch than to share the words overflowing from her heart, she reached up and gently touched his hair, marveling at how much it had grown since she had last seen him. "You do know it's growing back even thicker than before?"

"So they tell me," he said ruefully, unable to completely hide his pleasure as he ran his own hand over the flourishing crop of curls. "You may have to get used to it. It seems Dr. Evil has left the building. At least for now."

"Is that what your doctor told you?"

"That's what my lab results told him. They

looked even better than he had hoped. He didn't exactly tell me to rush out and buy my dream house, but he didn't rule out signing a long-term lease on a rental."

"Oh, Mark!" Abby didn't realize how relieved she was by his words until she actually staggered. She reached to throw her arms around his neck, hoping to rely on his strength until her own returned.

But he caught her by the shoulders and held her away from him, his warm hazel eyes searching her face with an intensity that made her feel even giddier. "Look, I appreciate everything you did for me while I was sick, but if you want to walk away now, I understand. Remission doesn't mean cured. I could still relapse somewhere down the road."

"And I could go out tomorrow and get hit by a bus." Abby beamed up at him through a haze of joyful tears. "Haven't you learned by now that there aren't any guarantees in this life?"

Mark lifted a hand to her cheek, touching her as if he still couldn't quite believe it was possible. "That's where you're wrong, Abby Donovan. Because I can guarantee that as long as there is breath in my body, I will love you."

Then he gathered her into his arms and kissed

her the way Sawyer kissed Kate for the very first time on *Lost*. The way Jack kissed Rose on the bow of the *Titanic*. The way Spike kissed Buffy at the end of the musical episode of *Buffy the Vampire Slayer*. He kissed her until all they could do was cling to each other, swaying to music only they could hear.

Somehow Abby knew it was a song that would last a lifetime, no matter how short or long their lives would be. If they could spend all of their todays together, she would gladly surrender all of her tomorrows.

When they finally drew apart, both as breathless as if they'd run the entire length of the Champs-Élysées, she was surprised to find the other diners still nibbling on their bread and cheese and smoking and nursing their glasses of wine. No one was staring at them or rolling their eyes or muttering beneath their breaths that the two of them should get a room.

And why would they? Paris was not only the City of Lights, but the City of Love.

"Are you sure this only counts as our third date?" Mark whispered into her hair, his breath warm against her ear. "I was thinking we might be able to count that night at the hospital when we snuck up to the rooftop terrace to watch the meteor shower and got locked out after the fire door closed."

Abby leaned back to smile up at him. "Get me an order of crème brûlée to go and I might even call it our fifth date."

Goodnight Tweetheart

Teresa Medeiros

Discussion Questions

1. When Mark and Abby first "meet" on Twitter, Mark isn't entirely truthful about his identity. Do you think it's common for people to wear "masks" when they first meet someone? To present themselves as the man or woman they believe the other person wants them to be?

2. What do you think about the statement Abby quotes to Mark during their first "date"?: "You'll never have more in common than you do on your first date."

3. Have you ever had immediate chemistry with someone you've met, either in a friendship or a romantic relationship? Do you believe it's a physical response or an emotional one?

4. Do you believe in love at first sight? Or love at first tweet?

5. Abby shares her favorite book, Peter S. Beagle's *A Fine and Private Place*, with Mark. Have you

ever found common ground with a stranger by sharing your favorite book, movie, TV show, or piece of music? Is that a mating ritual or just a common way that strangers often bond?

6. If you were to tell someone your favorite book at this precise moment in your life's journey, what would it be? How does it reflect who you are or your belief systems?

7. Abby says the central theme of *A Fine and Private Place* is that death gives life meaning and life gives death meaning. Do you believe this to be true?

8. Does life being finite give us even more reason to celebrate every moment of it? If you could do something special to celebrate your own life, what would it be?

9. How do you feel Abby's relationships with her parents colored her relationship with Mark?

10. Would you have been able to forgive Mark for his deception? Do you feel that Abby's response was appropriate? Would you have been harder on Mark or easier on him if faced with a similar circumstance?

11. Did you notice any hints about Mark's situation in their exchanges that Abby may have missed?

12. Abby and Mark both mention music in a way that tells you it's important to their lives. If you could pick out a song to reflect their relationship, what would it be? Have you and a significant other ever shared a special song you considered "yours"?

13. At one point Mark says, "Irving, like Jerry Seinfeld, knows the only way to survive this life is to view it as some sort of absurdist tragicomedy." Do you think he was being overly flippant or do you find that humor helps you cope with the challenges of your own life?

14. Do you believe that social media sites like Facebook and Twitter enhance intimacy or make it more difficult to achieve?

Continue reading for exclusive excerpts from
Teresa Medeiros's sizzling historical romances

The Devil Wears Plaid

and

The Pleasure of Your Kiss

plus an exciting sneak preview of

The Temptation of Your Touch

coming in early 2013 from Pocket Books

The Devil Wears Plaid

Teresa Medeiros

**Passion sparks in *USA Today* and *New York Times*
bestselling author Teresa Medeiros's irresistibly
tempting new Regency after a sexy Highlander
kidnaps his rival's spirited English bride . . .**

Emmaline Marlowe is about to wed the extremely
powerful laird of the Hepburn clan to save her father from debtor's prison when ruffian Jamie Sinclair bursts into the abbey on a magnificent black
horse and abducts her in one strong swoop.
Though he is Hepburn's sworn enemy, Emma's
mysterious captor is everything her bridegroom is
not—handsome, virile, dangerous . . . and a peril-
ous temptation for her yearning heart.

Jaime expects Emma to me some milksop English miss, not a fiery, defiant beauty whose irresistible charms will tempt him at every turn. But he
cannot allow either one of them to forget he is her
enemy and she his pawn in the deadly Highland
feud between the clans. So why does he still want
her so badly for himself? Stealing his enemy's bride
was simple, but can he claim her innocence without losing his heart?

Chapter One

*A*h, just look at the dear lass! She's all a'tremble with joy."

"And who could blame her? She's probably been dreamin' o' this day her entire life."

"Aye, 'tis every lass's dream, is it not? To wed a wealthy laird who can afford to grant her every wish?"

"She should consider herself blessed to have snared such an amazin' catch. With all those freckles, it's not as if she's any Great Beauty."

"I'd be willin' to wager she couldn't bleach them away with an entire jar o' Gowland's Lotion! And the copper shade o' her hair does make her look a wee bit common, don't you think? I heard the earl met her in London during her third and *final* Season when all hope o' findin' a husband had nearly been lost. Why, she's already one-and-twenty, they say."

"*No!* So turribly auld?"

"Aye, that's what I hear. She was on the verge o'

bein' placed firmly on the shelf, she was, until our laird spotted her sittin' with the confirmed spinsters and sent one o' his men o'er to dance with her."

Even as she gazed straight ahead and valiantly fought to ignore the avid whispers of the two women gossiping in the front pew of the abbey, Emmaline Marlowe could not deny the truth in their words.

She *had* been dreaming of this day her entire life.

She'd dreamed of standing before an altar and pledging her heart and her lifelong fidelity to the man she adored. She'd never caught a clear glimpse of his face in those misty dreams but there could be no denying the passion smoldering in his eyes as he vowed to love, honor and cherish her for the rest of his days.

She lowered her gaze to the quivering bouquet of dried heather in her hand, thankful the beaming onlookers who crowded the rows of long, narrow pews flanking the center aisle of the church were attributing her trembling to the joyful anticipation any eager young bride about to speak her vows might feel. She was the only one who knew it had more to do with the chill that seemed to permeate the ancient stones of the abbey.

And her heart.

She stole a glance at the churchyard beyond the tall, narrow windows. A sky the color of unpolished pewter brooded over the vale, making the day look more like deep winter than mid-April. The skeletal branches of oak and elm had yet to sprout a single bud of green. Crooked gravestones lurched out of the stony soil, their epitaphs worn away by the relentless assault of wind and rain. Emma wondered how many of those who now slumbered beneath the ground had once been brides like her, young women full of hopes and dreams dashed too soon by choices made by others and the inescapable march of time.

The jagged crags of the mountain loomed over the churchyard like monuments to an even more primitive age. These harsh Highland climes where winter refused to yield its stubborn grip seemed a world away from the gently rolling hills of Lancashire where she and her sisters loved to romp with such careless abandon. Those hills were already green and tender with the promise of spring, beckoning home any wanderer foolish enough to forsake them.

Home, Emma thought, her heart seized by a sharp pang of longing. A place she would no longer belong after today.

She shot a panicked glance over her shoulder to find her parents sitting in the Hepburn family pew, beaming proudly at her through eyes glazed with tears. She was a good girl. A dutiful daughter. The one they had always relied upon to set a sound example for her three younger sisters. Elberta, Edwina and Ernestine were huddled together on the pew next to their mother, dabbing at their swollen eyes with their own handkerchiefs. If Emma could have convinced herself it was happiness that prompted her family's weeping, their tears might have been easier to bear.

More simpering whispers intruded upon her thoughts as the women resumed their conversation. "Just look at him! He still cuts a strikin' figure, doesn't he?"

"Indeed! It does one's heart proud. And you can tell he already dotes upon the lass."

No longer able to deny the inevitability of her fate, Emma turned back to the altar and lifted her eyes to meet the adoring gaze of her bridegroom.

Then lowered them as she remembered she towered over his wizened form by over half a foot.

He grinned up at her, nearly dislodging the poorly fitted set of Wedgwood china teeth from his mouth. His cheeks all but disappeared as he sucked the teeth back in with a pop that seemed to echo through the abbey with the force of a gunshot. Emma swallowed, hoping the cataracts that clouded his rheumy blue eyes would render his vision poor enough to mistake her grimace of distaste for a smile.

His withered form was draped with the full regalia befitting his station as laird of the Hepburn lands and chieftain of Clan Hepburn. A billowing red and black plaid nearly swallowed his hunched shoulders. The matching tailored kilt exposed knees as bony as a pair of ivory doorknobs. A mangy sporran hung between his legs, the ceremonial purse balding in uneven patches just like his skull.

The two gossiping old biddies were right, Emma reminded herself sternly. The man was an earl—an extremely powerful nobleman rumored to have both the respect of his peers and the ear of the king.

It was her duty to her family—and their rapidly dwindling fortunes—to accept the earl's suit. After all, it wasn't her papa's fault he had been cursed with a passel of daughters instead of being blessed with sons who could have gone out and made their own fortunes in the world. Emma's catching the Earl of Hepburn's eye just before donning the drab mantle of spinsterhood had been a stroke of extraordinary good luck for them all. Thanks to the generous settlement the earl had already bestowed upon her father, her mother and sisters would never again have to be startled from their sleep by the terrifying racket of creditors banging on the front door of their ramshackle manor house or spend their every waking moment in fear of being carted off to the workhouse.

Emma might be the prettiest Marlowe girl among her sisters, but she was not so attractive that she could afford to turn down such an illustrious suitor. During their grueling journey to this isolated corner of the Highlands, her mother had discussed every detail of her upcoming nuptials with determined good cheer. When they reached the rolling foothills and the earl's home had finally come into view, her sisters had dutifully gasped with admiration, not realizing their pretended envy was more painful to Emma than overt pity.

No one could deny the splendor of the ancient castle nestled beneath the shadow of the lofty, snowcapped crag of Ben Nevis—a castle that had welcomed the Hepburn lords and their brides for centuries. When this day was done, Emma would be its mistress as well as the earl's bride.

As she blinked down at her bridegroom, she struggled to transform her grimace into a genuine smile. The old man had been the very soul of kindness to her and her family ever since spotting her across that crowded public assembly room during one of the last balls of the Season. Instead of sending an emissary on his behalf, he had traveled all the way to Lancashire himself to court her and seek her papa's blessing.

He had conducted himself like a true nobleman during his calls, never once making a disparaging remark about their shabby drawing room with its faded carpet, peeling wallpaper and mismatched furniture, or casting a contemptuous eye over her own outmoded and much-darned gowns. Judging by his courtly charm and gracious demeanor, one would have thought he was taking tea at Carlton House with the Prince Regent.

He had treated Emma as if she were already a countess, not the eldest daughter of an impoverished baronet one ill-considered wager away from the poorhouse. And he had never once arrived empty-handed. A stern-faced footman always followed one step behind the earl, his burly arms laden with gifts—hand-painted fans, glass bugle beads and colorful fashion plates for Emma's sisters; French-milled lavender-scented soap and handsome bolts of muslin and dimity for her mother; bottles of the finest Scotch whisky for her papa; and leather-bound editions of William Blake's *Songs of Innocence* or Fanny Burney's latest novel for Emma herself. They might have been only trinkets to a man of the earl's means, but such luxuries had been in scarce supply around the manor house for a very long time. His generosity had brought a flush of pleasure to her mother's wan cheeks and elicited genuine shrieks of delight from Emma's sisters.

Emma owed the man her gratitude and her loyalty, if not her heart.

Besides, how long could he possibly live? she thought with a desperate twinge of guilt.

Although the earl was rumored to be nearly eighty years of age, he looked closer to one hundred and fifty. Judging by his grayish pallor and the consumptive hiccup marring each of his breaths, he might not even survive their wedding night. As a fetid blast of that breath wafted to her nostrils, Emma swayed on her feet, fearing she might not survive it either.

Almost as if she had read Emma's grim thoughts, one of the women sitting on the front pew whispered primly, "One thing you can say about our laird—he ought to have ample experience in pleasin' a woman."

Her companion failed to smother a rather porcine snort. "Indeed he should. Especially since he's already outlived three wives and all the bairns they produced, not to mention a gaggle o' mistresses."

The image of her elderly bridegroom gumming her lips in a fumbling parody of passion sent a fresh shudder coursing down Emma's spine. She still hadn't quite recovered from having to sit through her mother's painfully earnest instructions on what would be expected of her on the wedding night. As if the act described hadn't been horrid or humiliating enough, her mother had also informed her that if she turned her face away and wriggled a bit beneath him, the earl's exertions would be over that much more quickly. If his attentions became too arduous, she was to close her eyes and think of something pleasant—like a particularly lovely sunrise or a tin of fresh sugar biscuits. Once he was finished with her, she would be free to tug down the hem of her nightdress and go to sleep.

Free, Emma's heart echoed with a throb of despair. After this day she would never be free again.

She averted her eyes from her groom's hopeful face to find the earl's great-nephew glowering at her. Ian Hepburn was the only person in the abbey who looked as unhappy as she felt. With his high Roman brow, dimpled chin and sleek dark hair gathered at the nape in a satin queue, he should have been a handsome man. But on this day the classical beauty of his features was tainted by an emotion dangerously close to hatred. He did not approve of this match, no doubt fearing her nubile young body would produce a new Hepburn heir and deprive him of his inheritance.

As the minister droned on, reading from the

Book of Common Order, Emma looked over her shoulder again to see her mother turn her face into her papa's coat as if she could no longer bear to watch the proceedings. Her sisters were beginning to sniffle more loudly by the minute. Ernestine's sharp little nose was as pink as a rabbit's, and judging by the violent quiver of Edwina's plump bottom lip, it was only a matter of time before she broke into full-fledged sobs.

Soon the minister's ramblings would draw to a close, leaving Emma with no choice but to pledge her devotion and her body to this shriveled stranger.

She cast a wild-eyed glance behind her, wondering what they would all do if she lifted the lace-trimmed hem of her silk wedding dress and made a mad dash for the door. She'd heard numerous cautionary tales of careless travelers disappearing into the Highland wilderness, never to be seen or heard from again. At the moment, it sounded like a wonderfully tempting prospect. After all, it wasn't as if her decrepit groom could chase her down, toss her over his shoulder and haul her back to the altar.

As if to underscore that fact, the earl began to croak out his vows. Too soon, he was done and the minister was looking expectantly at her.

As was everyone else in the abbey.

As her silence dragged on, one of the women murmured, "Och, the puir lass is overcome with emotion."

"If she swoons, he'll naught be able to catch her without breakin' his back," her companion whispered.

Emma opened her mouth, then closed it again. It had gone as dry as cotton, forcing her to wet her lips with the tip of her tongue before she made another attempt at speech. The minister blinked at her from behind his steel-rimmed spectacles, the compassion in his kind brown eyes bringing her dangerously near to tears.

Emma glanced over her shoulder again, but this time it wasn't her mother or her sisters who captured her gaze; it was her papa.

There was no mistaking the pleading look in his eyes. Eyes the exact same dusky blue shade as hers. Eyes that had for too long looked both haunted and hunted. She would almost swear the tremor in his hands had decreased since the earl had signed over the settlement. She hadn't seen him reach for the flask he always kept tucked in his waistcoat pocket even once since she'd accepted the earl's proposal.

In his encouraging smile, she caught a glimpse of another man—a younger man with clear eyes and steady hands whose breath smelled of peppermint instead of spirits. He would swoop down and whisk her up to his shoulders for a dizzying ride, making her feel as if she were queen of all she surveyed instead of just a grubby toddler with skinned knees and a snaggle-toothed smile.

She also saw something in her father's eyes that she hadn't seen for a very long time—hope.

Emma turned back to her bridegroom, squaring her shoulders. Despite what the onlookers might believe, she had no intention of weeping or swooning. She had always prided herself on being made of sterner stuff than that. If she must marry this earl to secure the future and fortunes of her family, then marry him she would. And she would strive to be the best wife and countess his wealth—and title—could buy.

She was opening her mouth—fully prepared to promise to love, cherish and obey him, for better or worse, in sickness and in health, till death did them part—when the double doors of iron-banded oak at the rear of the abbey came crashing open, letting in a blast of wintry air and a dozen armed men.

The abbey erupted in a chorus of startled shrieks and gasps. The men fanned out among the pews, their unshaven faces grim with determination, their pistols held at the ready to quell any sign of resistance.

Instead of fear, Emma felt a ridiculous flare of hope ignite in her heart.

As the initial outcry subsided, Ian Hepburn boldly stepped into the center aisle of the abbey, placing himself between the forbidding mouths of the intruders' weapons and his great-uncle. "What is the meaning of this?" he shouted, his clipped tones ringing from the vaulted ceiling. "Have you savages no respect for the house of the Lord?"

"And which lord would that be?" a man responded in a Scots burr so deep and rich it sent an involuntary shiver down Emma's spine. "The one who formed these mountains with His own hands or the one who believes he was born with the right to rule them?"

She gasped along with everyone else as the owner of that voice rode a towering black horse right through the doorway of the abbey. A shocked murmur went up as the wedding guests shrank back into their pews, their avid gazes reflecting equal parts fear and fascination. Oddly enough, Emma's gaze wasn't transfixed by the magnificent beast with its gleaming barreled chest and flowing ebony mane but by the man straddling the steed's imposing back.

Thick, sable wings of hair framed his sun-bronzed face, presenting a startling contrast to the frosty green of his eyes. Despite the chill of the day, he wore only a green and black woolen kilt, a pair of lace-up boots, and a sleeveless vest of beaten brown leather that exposed his broad, smooth chest to the elements. He handled the beast as if he'd been born to the saddle, his powerful shoulders and well-muscled forearms barely showing a strain as he guided the horse right up the aisle, forcing Ian to stumble backward or be trampled by the animal's deadly hooves.

From beside her, Emma heard the earl hiss, *"Sinclair!"*

She turned to find her elderly groom's face suffused with color and twisted with hatred. Judging by the ripe, purple vein pulsing in his temple, he might not survive the wedding, much less the wedding night.

"Forgive me for interrupting such a tender moment," the intruder said without so much as a trace of remorse as he reined his mount to a prancing halt halfway down the aisle. "Surely you didn't think I could resist dropping by to pay my respects on such a momentous occasion. My invitation must have been lost in the post."

The earl shook one palsied fist at him. "The only invitation any Sinclair is likely to receive from me is a writ of arrest from the magistrate and a date with the hangman."

In reaction to the threat, the man simply arched

one bemused eyebrow. "I had such high hopes that the next time I darkened the door of this abbey, it would be for your funeral, not another wedding. But you always have been a randy auld goat. I should have known you couldn't resist buying another bride to warm your bed."

For the first time since he'd muscled his way into the abbey, the stranger's mocking gaze flicked toward her. Even that brief glance was enough to bring a stinging flush to Emma's fair cheeks, especially since his words held the undeniable and damning ring of truth.

This time it was almost a relief when Ian Hepburn once again sought to impose himself between them. "You may mock us and pretend to be avenging your ancestors as you always do," he said, a sneer curling his upper lip, "but everyone on this mountain knows that the Sinclairs have never been anything more than common cutthroats and thieves. If you and your ruffians have come to divest my uncle's guests of their jewels and purses, then why don't you bloody well get on with it and stop wasting your breath and our time?"

With surprising strength, Emma's groom shoved his way past her, nearly sending her sprawling. "I don't need my nephew to fight my battles. I'm not afraid of an insolent whelp like you, Jamie

Sinclair," he snarled, marching right past his nephew with one bony fist still upraised. "Do your worst!"

"Oh, I haven't come for you, auld mon." A lazy smile curved the intruder's lips as he drew a gleaming black pistol from the waistband of his kilt and pointed it at the snowy white bodice of Emma's gown. "I've come for your bride."

Chapter Two

As Emma gazed into the stranger's glacial green eyes over the mouth of his pistol, it suddenly occurred to her that there might be worse fates than agreeing to wed a doddering old man. The thick, sooty lashes framing those eyes did nothing to veil the unspoken threat glittering in their depths.

At the sight of the pistol pointed at Emma's breast, her mother clapped a hand over her mouth to muffle a broken cry. Elberta and Edwina clutched at each other, the clusters of silk violets on their matching bonnets trembling and their blue eyes wide with shock, while Ernestine began to paw through her reticule for her smelling salts.

Her father leapt to his feet but made no move to leave the pew. It was as if he was frozen in place by some force more powerful than his devotion to his daughter. "I say, man," he barked, steadying his hands on the back of the pew in front of him, "what in the devil is the meaning of this?"

While the minister backed toward the altar, deliberately distancing himself from Emma, the earl lowered his clenched fist and slowly shuffled backward, leaving a clear path between Emma's heart and the loaded pistol. Judging by the expectant hush that had fallen over the rest of the guests, she and Sinclair might have been the only two souls in the abbey. Emma supposed some response was required of her as well—that she ought to swoon or burst into tears or plead prettily for her life.

Knowing that was exactly what the villain probably expected her to do gave her the courage to tamp down her own budding terror and stand straight and tall, to lift her chin and meet his ruthless gaze with a defiant glare of her own. She dug her fingernails into the bouquet to hide the violent quaking of her hands, crushing the lingering perfume of the heather from the crisp blooms. For an elusive second, another emotion flickered through those frosty green eyes—one that might have been amusement . . . or admiration.

It was Ian Hepburn's turn to march past his uncle, his dark eyes smoldering with contempt. He stopped a healthy distance from the man on horseback. "So now you've sunk to defiling churches *and* threatening to shoot helpless, unarmed women. I suppose I should have expected no better from a bastard like you, *Sin*," he added, hissing the nickname as if it were the vilest of epithets.

Sinclair briefly shifted his gaze from Emma to Ian, his grip on the pistol unwavering. "Then you're not to be disappointed, are you, auld friend?"

"I'm not your friend!" Ian shouted.

"No," Sinclair replied softly, his voice tinged with what might have been either bitterness or regret. "I suppose you never were."

Even in retreat, the earl remained defiant. "You're living proof that it takes more than studying at St. Andrews to turn a mountain rat into a gentleman! It must gall your grandfather beyond measure to know that sending you off to university was such a waste of his precious coins. Coins no doubt stolen from my own coffers by his motley band of rabble!"

The earl's insults didn't seem to faze Sinclair. "I wouldn't exactly call it a waste. If I hadn't gone to St. Andrews, I might have never made the acquaintance of your charming nephew here." That earned him a fresh glare from Ian. "But I will make sure to give my grandfather your regards the next time I see him."

So this brigand had lived among civilized folk for a time. That would explain why the roughest edges had been polished off his burr, leaving it even more dangerously silky and musical to Emma's ears.

"Just what do you plan to do, you miserable pup?" the earl demanded. "Have you come to hasten your own inevitable journey to hell by murdering my bride in cold blood on the altar of a church?"

Emma was alarmed to note that her devoted bridegroom didn't look particularly dismayed by the prospect. With his title and riches, she supposed it would be a simple enough matter for him to procure another bride. Ernestine and Elberta were both nearly old enough to wed. Perhaps her father would be allowed to keep the earl's settlement if he offered the man a choice between the two girls so the ceremony could proceed without further interruption.

After they'd mopped up her blood, of course.

A nervous hiccup of a giggle escaped her. She had avoided swooning or begging for her life only to end up skating dangerously near to hysteria. It was just beginning to occur to her that she might actually die here at the hands of this merciless stranger—a virgin bride never knowing true passion or the adoring touch of a lover.

"Unlike some," Sinclair said with pointed politeness, "I'm not in the habit of murdering innocent women." A tender smile curved his lips, more dangerous somehow than any sneer or glower. "I said I'd come for your bride, Hepburn, not that I'd come to kill her."

Emma read his intent a heartbeat before anyone else in the abbey. It was there in the squaring of his unshaven jaw, the tension that rippled through his muscular thighs, the way his powerful fists wrapped around the beaten leather of the reins.

Yet all she could do was stand rooted to the flagstones, paralyzed by the raw determination in his narrowed gaze.

Everything seemed to happen at once. Sinclair dug his heels into the horse's flanks. The beast lurched forward, eyes rolling wildly, nostrils flaring. It came charging down the aisle of the abbey, heading straight for Emma. Her mother let out a bloodcurdling scream, then slumped into a dead faint. The minister dove behind the altar, his black robes flapping behind him like the wings of a crow. Emma flung her arms up over her face, bracing herself to be trampled beneath those flashing hooves.

At the last possible second, the horse veered to the left while Sinclair leaned right. He wrapped one powerful arm around Emma's waist and swept her into the air, tossing her belly-down across his lap as if she weighed no more than a sack of wormy potatoes and knocking the air clear out of her. She was still struggling to catch her breath when he wheeled the horse in a tight circle, forcing the beast up on its hind legs for a dizzying pirouette. As those deadly hooves pawed at the air, Emma sucked in a breath that was sure to be her last as she waited for the horse to topple over backward and crush them both.

But her captor had other ideas. He sawed at the reins with brute strength, using sheer mastery to force the creature to succumb to his will. The beast let out an earsplitting whinny. Its front hooves came crashing down, its iron shoes striking sparks off the flagstones.

Sinclair's strong voice carried, even over the shrill shrieks and frantic shouts of alarm echoing off the vaulted ceiling. But his words were meant for the earl alone. "If you want her back unharmed, Hepburn, you'll have to pay and pay dearly! For your own sins and the sins o' your fathers. I'll not return her to you until you return to me what's rightfully mine."

Then he snapped the reins on the horse's back, sending the beast charging back down the aisle of the abbey. They thundered through the doorway and past the crooked gravestones of the churchyard, each of the horse's long, powerful strides carrying Emma farther away from any hope of rescue.

The Pleasure of Your Kiss

Teresa Medeiros

"Few authors have Medeiros's storytelling talents"
(*RT Book Reviews*), which are on full display in
this swashbuckling romance that tempts readers
from the exotic intrigues of a sultan's court to the
glittering ballrooms of Regency London.

Legendary adventurer Ashton Burke has roamed
the globe for ten years trying to forget the spirited
woman he left behind in England. His devil-may-
care pursuits are interrupted, though, when he reluctantly agrees to retrieve his brother's kidnapped
fiancée from a sultan's harem. Too late, he discovers
his quarry is none other than Clarinda Cardew, the
very same girl who made off with his jaded heart.

The last thing Clarinda wants is to be trapped
in a palace of sensual delights with the man whose
irresistible kisses still haunt her sleepless nights.
She quickly realizes that allowing Ashton to rescue
her may put her yearning heart in even greater
peril. In a journey both tantalizing and treacherous, Ashton and Clarinda resume the impetuous
steps of their dangerous dance only to discover the
most seductive pleasure of all may be love itself.

Chapter One

*O*h, Clarinda! Have you seen the latest edition of the *Snitch*? I picked one up at the docks before we sailed and there's an absolutely delicious article about Captain Sir Ashton Burke!"

Clarinda Cardew felt her fingers tighten involuntarily, biting into the leather binding of the book she was reading. Despite the balmy warmth of the sea breeze caressing her cheeks, she could feel her face freezing into the mask of calculated disinterest it always wore whenever That Name was mentioned. She didn't require a mirror to know how effective it was. She'd had nine long years to perfect it.

"Indeed?" she murmured without lifting her eyes from the page.

Unfortunately, Poppy was too enamored of her subject matter to notice Clarinda's marked lack of encouragement. Adjusting the wire-rimmed spectacles perched on the tip of her nose, Poppy leaned forward in her deck chair. "According to this article, he's fluent in over fifteen languages, including French, Italian, Latin, Arabic, and Sanskrit, and has spent most of the last decade journeying from one corner of the globe to the other."

"Strictly speaking," Clarinda said drily, "globes don't have corners. They're round."

Undaunted, Poppy continued, "'After leading his regiment in the East India Company army to a stunning victory in the Burmese war, he was awarded a knighthood by the king. Based on his ferocious skill in single combat, the men under his command gave him the nickname Sir Savage.'"

"So much more intimidating than Sir Unfailingly Polite." Feeling rather savage herself, Clarinda flicked to the next page of her book and stared blindly down at words that might as well have been written in Sanskrit or some other ancient tongue.

"'Rumor has it that while he was in India, he rescued a beautiful Hindustani princess from the bandits who had kidnapped her from her palace. When her father offered him her hand in marriage and a fortune in gold and jewels as a reward, Burke informed him that he would be content with nothing more than a kiss.'"

"Her father must have been a most excellent kisser," Clarinda replied, lifting the book to hide her face altogether.

Poppy dragged her rapt gaze away from the *Snitch* long enough to give Clarinda an exasperated glance. "Not from her father, silly. From the princess. According to the article, Captain Burke's romantic exploits are nearly as legendary as his military ones. It says here that after requesting a discharge from the army, Burke was engaged by the African Association to lead an expedition deep into the continent's interior. His alliance with the association was severed three years ago when he returned from Africa with copious notes on the carnal habits of the primitive tribes he discovered there. Even the most sophisticated of scholars were scandalized by the attention to detail evidenced by his findings. Some of them even dared to suggest he might have participated in these rituals himself!"

Clarinda winced as Poppy's scandalized titter threatened to pierce her eardrums. The image of a man lowering himself into the sleek arms of some ebony-skinned beauty while flames leapt around them and native drums beat out an irresistible rhythm made her own temples begin to throb. She briefly considered throwing the scandal sheet overboard. Or perhaps even Poppy herself.

Normally Penelope Montmorency, known as Poppy to both Clarinda and to their former classmates from Miss Bedelia Throckmorton's Seminary for Young Ladies, was a most amiable companion. She might be overly fond of society gossip and iced tea-cakes and have a tendency to speak as if her every utterance was punctuated by an exclamation mark, but she was also good-natured and loyal, without an ounce of genuine malice in her short, plump frame.

Poppy was usually content to read to Clarinda from the sacred pages of the *Ladies' Fashionable Repository*. But Clarinda supposed the ornate plumes, stuffed birds, and clusters of ribbons the French were wearing on the brims of their bonnets that summer couldn't hope to compare to the legendary exploits—romantic or otherwise—of the dashing Captain Sir Ashton Burke.

The gentle pitch and roll of the ship's deck beneath their chairs no longer felt soothing to Clarinda's nerves. Although she'd never suffered so much as a twinge of seasickness, she was starting to feel distinctly queasy. Hoping to ease the sensation, she set aside her book, rose from the deck chair, and made her way forward to the bow of the ship. Although there was nothing but sea and sky as far as the eye could see, there was still nowhere she could go to escape Poppy's fascination with the subject of the article.

"'Since severing his ties with both the East India Company and the African Association,'" her companion read, "'the aura of mystery surrounding Burke has only deepened. There are some who speculate he now spends his time acquiring priceless archaeological treasures or that some foreign government may have even engaged his services as a spy.'"

Clarinda forced a yawn. "He must not be particularly adept at it if everyone suspects he's a spy."

"The article even includes a sketched likeness of him." There was a cheerful rustling as Poppy turned the scandal sheet this way and that, studying it from every possible angle before announcing with great conviction, "I fear the artist must have flattered him. No man could possibly be *that* good-looking, could he?"

Clarinda clutched the ship's railing, fighting the temptation to whirl around and snatch the newspaper from Poppy's hands. She didn't need a sketch to remember amber irises rimmed in black and flecked with sparks of the purest gold, a devil-may-care dimple slashed in one lean cheek, beautifully sculpted lips that always seemed to be on the verge of quirking in a teasing smile before softening to steal a kiss . . . or a defenseless heart. Perhaps Michelangelo or Raphael could have done justice to those details, but it would be impossible for a few careless strokes of a pen to capture the irresistible vitality of such a man.

"He may have been absent from England for many years, but you grew up on adjoining estates, did you not?" Poppy asked. "Surely you must have caught at least a glimpse of him."

"It's been years since I laid eyes on him and he was little more than a lad then. My recollection has grown somewhat hazy," Clarinda lied. "But I do vaguely seem to remember a long, hooked nose, a pair of spindly bowlegs, and protruding teeth like a beaver's." It took Clarinda a moment to realize she had just described their least favorite dancing master from their days at Miss Throckmorton's. Poor Mr. Tudbury had also had an unfortunate tendency to spray spittle when snapping out commands for them to pirouette or perform a *battement glissé*.

Poppy sighed wistfully. "I wonder where the captain might have disappeared to this time. Do you suppose he's gone off to rescue more princesses?"

Betrayed by the treacherous twinge of yearning her friend's mooning had stirred in her own heart, Clarinda swung around to face her. "Really, Poppy! There's no need to fawn over the man as if we were both still a pair of simpering schoolgirls! He's nothing but a greedy soldier of fortune who makes his living robbing tombs and selling his sword to the highest bidder. The press may choose to glorify him but that doesn't make him a hero." Clarinda dampened the smoldering fuse of her temper with a cool sniff. "Most men who cloak themselves in rumor and innuendo do so because there is nothing of real substance to hide. They spread these tall tales themselves simply to cover up their own . . . *shortcomings*."

"Shortcomings?" Poppy's periwinkle blue eyes widened behind the thick lenses of her spectacles. "Surely you don't mean . . ." The corkscrewed clusters of apricot-tinted curls gathered at her temples danced like the ears of a spaniel as she clapped a plump hand over her mouth to smother a shocked giggle. "Why, Clarinda, you wicked thing! You must learn to mind that naughty tongue of yours. After all, you'll be the wife of an earl in less than a fortnight!"

Poppy's chiding words reminded Clarinda of exactly what—and who—awaited her at the end of their journey through the choppy waters of the North Atlantic. She hardly needed Poppy to remind her she was the envy of every eager young debutante and scheming mama whose hopes had been crushed by the recent announcement of her engagement. She had somehow managed to snare England's most eligible bachelor—and one of its most beloved sons—at the relatively advanced age of twenty-six.

Her fiancé was a marvelous man—handsome, kind, intelligent, and noble in both name and character. He was everything a woman should want.

Which didn't explain the hollow ache in Clarinda's heart as she turned back to the sea to escape Poppy's teasing gaze. Or her desperate desire to tear off her wide-brimmed hat, pluck out her mother-of-pearl hair combs, and let the wind have its way with her long wheaten tresses.

The sun shimmered off the crest of the distant swells, its uncompromising brightness stinging her eyes. "When I am a countess," she said with determined cheer, "I shall never have to curb my tongue again. Instead, I shall expect everyone around me to curb theirs."

"Beginning with me, I suppose." Poppy tossed the scandal sheet aside and rose to join her at the rail. "I would have thought you'd be more interested in Captain Burke's adventures, especially since he is about to become your—"

"Let's talk of something else, shall we?" Clarinda interrupted before Poppy could speak the unspeakable and drive her to throw herself overboard. "Like how you're going to be the toast of the regiment once we arrive in Burma."

"Do you really think so?" A glow of pleasure suffused the ripe apples of Poppy's cheeks. "I do so fancy soldiers! It's always been my opinion that a uniform can make even the plainest of gentlemen look like a prince and a hero!"

"Just you wait and see. Handsome young officers will be engaging in fisticuffs and challenging each other to duels, all for the privilege of standing in line to fill out your dance card." Clarinda had every intention of making good on that promise. Even if her new husband had to order the men in his employ to do so upon threat of court-martial ... or execution.

"But what if word of my"—Poppy threw a nervous glance over her shoulder and lowered her voice to a stage whisper, as if some gossip-minded old biddy could be lurking behind the oaken barrels lashed to the bulkhead—"*indiscretion* has already reached the ears of some of the officers' wives through the post?"

It was one of the unfathomable ironies of life that a shy, mild-mannered creature like Poppy had unwittingly gotten herself embroiled in the scandal of the season. One that had set jaws to dropping and tongues to wagging from London to Surrey and effectively destroyed her last hope of landing a husband before she was placed firmly on the shelf.

Clarinda's own jaw had dropped when she had first heard Poppy had been caught in a worse-than-compromising position with a certain young gentleman from Berwickshire. She had dismissed the torrid tale as so much rubbish until she learned there had been more than a dozen witnesses to the incident. Unable to bear the thought of Poppy being condemned for a sin she had not committed, she had immediately packed a portmanteau and gone rushing to her friend's rescue, just as she had so many times at the Seminary when the wealthier, prettier girls were mocking Poppy's ill-fitting bodices and thick spectacles or calling her Piggy instead of Poppy.

Poppy, the only daughter of a humble country squire, had always been absurdly grateful for Clarinda's patronage, but Clarinda was equally grateful for Poppy's stalwart friendship. Clarinda's papa had been eager for her to get a first-rate education, but the first thing she had learned at Miss Throckmorton's establishment was that money couldn't buy the esteem of those who fancied themselves superior by birth. When the budding little "ladies" had discovered Clarinda's papa had made his fortune in trade, they had turned up their patrician noses and openly mocked her lineage . . . or lack thereof. By turning up her own nose and pretending their cruel words and petty slights didn't cut her to the quick, she had eventually earned their respect and ended up being one of the most popular girls at the school.

But she had never forgotten that Poppy had been her first and truest friend or that they had originally been drawn together because neither of them had fit in.

Clarinda was trusting the outpost at Burma would be ripe with lonely officers desperate for female companionship. Women of gentle breeding would be scarce, and past indiscretions would be more likely to be forgiven and forgotten instead of dwelled upon with malice and relish.

In their own way, she supposed she and Poppy were each fleeing England and its memories, both good and bad.

"Any officer—or gentleman—who wouldn't dismiss such idle gossip isn't worthy to polish the boots of Miss Penelope Montmorency," she assured her friend, "much less seek her hand in matrimony."

Poppy's smile reappeared, dimpling her cheeks. "I'm only hoping I can find a man half as passionate and devoted as yours. I think it's terribly romantic that he would arrange passage for you on one of his own ships so you could travel halfway around the world to become his bride."

Passion was never a word Clarinda had really equated with her fiancé. True, he had been pursuing her for a long time, but his proposal had consisted of a detailed list of all the reasons why they would suit, not an ardent declaration of love. Yet the steadfastness of his nature had finally convinced her he would never leave her to go chasing after some foolish dream.

Her shrug indicated a lightness of heart she did not feel. "The earl is both devoted and practical. His position within the Company carries with it tremendous responsibilities. I can hardly expect him to abandon his duties and return to London for something as frivolous as a wedding." Linking her arm through Poppy's, she turned her face toward the wind, relishing its promise of freedom, even if it was only an illusion. "I can't begin to tell you what a comfort it is to have you by my side on this journey. I suggest we both stop fretting over the past and the future and start savoring every moment of this voyage. It may very well be our last grand adventure before we settle down into a life of dull respectability."

Clarinda was proved wrong with her very next breath when thunder boomed down from the clear blue sky. She and Poppy barely had time to turn their bewildered glances toward its cloudless vault before something struck the water in front of the ship with a tremendous splash, drenching them both in chill salt spray.

"What in the devil...?" Clarinda muttered,

thankful she hadn't yet given up cursing in preparation for her new station in life.

Before she could mop the water from her eyes, another boom sounded, followed by a deafening crack from behind them. They whirled around just in time to see the towering mainmast of the ship begin to topple sideways like a felled tree, its mighty trunk splintered by the deadly weight of a cannonball. Clarinda was vaguely aware of Poppy's fingernails biting into the tender skin of her forearm, but all she could do was watch in helpless horror as what looked like acres of sail came billowing down to bury the deck in a canvas shroud.

They were forced to let go of each other and grasp the rail behind them as the ship lurched to the left, its forward momentum demolished along with its mainmast. Hoarse shouts assailed their ears, underscored by the high-pitched keening of some poor soul in agonizing pain. Sailors came pouring across the deck from every direction, some bearing buckets of water, others dropping to their knees to beat at the smoldering topsail with their bare hands.

As the vessel began to list in a stomach-churning circle, effectively crippled by that one deadly blow, a young lieutenant came racing toward them from the aftercastle of the ship. "Please, ladies, you must get belowdecks immediately! We're under attack!"

"Attack?" Clarinda echoed, his frantic words only deepening her confusion. As far as she knew, there was no one left to attack them. Since the final defeat of Napoléon's navy, most of England's enemies had been routed and subdued, if not by sword and cannon, then by various treaties. No one had dared to challenge England's supremacy on the high seas in nearly two decades.

The sailor stumbled to a halt in front of them and snatched off his bicorne hat, remembering his manners even at such a trying time. "I'm afraid it's pirates, miss." His Adam's apple bobbed in his throat as he made a valiant attempt to swallow his own terror. "Corsairs."

Poppy gasped. One had only to whisper that name to strike terror in the heart of even the most courageous of souls. Parents had been using it to chasten generations of rebellious children, whispering in their little ears that the notorious pirates would come and snatch them from their beds in the dead of night if they failed to recite their evening prayers or eat every last spoonful of their porridge.

The Corsairs had always been notorious for prowling the Mediterranean waters. They would sack every ship they encountered for its booty, none so valuable as the women they captured and sold at the barbarian slave markets in North Africa and Arabia.

And those were the lucky ones.

"I don't understand." Clarinda clenched her teeth to still their sudden chattering. "I thought the French subdued the Corsairs when they conquered Algiers."

"Most of them did surrender at that time. But that only made the ones who refused more desperate and ruthless." The lieutenant darted a glance at the growing chaos behind him. "Please, miss, we haven't much time to get you the two of you out of harm's way." His voice cracked, betraying both his youth and how near he was to succumbing to panic himself. "If they board us . . ."

There was no need for him to finish. Nor did Clarinda have the heart to point out that if the Corsairs succeeded in boarding the ship, there would be nowhere she and Poppy—or any of the other women on the ship, including the captain's wife and their own maids—could hide to escape the pirates' brutal clutches.

She closed her fingers around Poppy's trembling hand, dredging up a reassuring smile from the reserves of her faltering courage. "Come, my dear. It seems we're about to embark upon a much grander adventure than we anticipated."

The lieutenant drew his pistol and started back across the deck, gesturing for them to follow. They raced after him, hand in hand like two frightened little girls. They were halfway to the narrow passageway that would carry them deep into the tenuous safety of the hold when Clarinda stumbled to a halt.

Giving Poppy an apologetic look, she wrenched her hand free and went flying back across the deck.

"Clarinda!" Poppy screamed, terror ripening in her voice. *What are you doing?*

"Proving myself a sentimental fool," Clarinda muttered under her breath.

The scandal sheet still lay beside the chair where Poppy had so carelessly tossed it. As Clarinda snatched up the page with the likeness of Captain Burke sketched upon it, a round of pistol fire erupted from somewhere on the ship, followed by the ringing clash of steel against steel.

She wheeled around and went racing back to her friend's side, yanking the breathless Poppy into a dead run to make up for every step of the ground they had lost. She had no intention of letting anyone else suffer for her folly. The lieutenant had just wrenched open the hatch and was frantically waving them toward the shadowy mouth of the passageway. They had nearly reached him when his expression underwent a startling transformation.

His mouth went slack. He gave Clarinda a bewildered look, as if someone had made a joke at his expense that he didn't quite comprehend.

Then he slowly lowered his gaze to his chest.

That was when Clarinda saw the tip of the silvery blade protruding from the center of it.

Poppy let out a bloodcurdling scream. As the lieutenant pitched forward, Clarinda started toward him, instinctively trying to break his fall. But as she reached for him, that same long, curved blade was wrenched from his back and brandished in their direction. The lieutenant collapsed to the deck in a bloody heap, leaving the two of them all alone to face half a dozen men armed with pistols and scimitars. Their turbans and flowing robes were already spattered with blood, little of it their own.

Her breath shortening to terrified pants, Clarinda began to back away from them, dragging the paralyzed Poppy along with her. She gave the ill-fated young lieutenant one last look, but from the blood trickling from the corner of his mouth and the mist already claiming his eyes, clearly he was beyond anyone's help. He looked even younger in death than he had in life. Clarinda's savage regret that she hadn't at least been allowed to cradle his head in her lap as he died coalesced into a fierce urge to protect and survive.

Thrusting Poppy behind her, she reached up to the brim of her hat and whipped out the only weapon at her disposal. She thrust the pearl-tipped hatpin toward the advancing men. "Stay away from us, you miserable brigands. Or I'll run you through, I will!"

The men might not have understood her words, but there was no mistaking the murderous look in her eye. The hulking giant gripping the bloody scimitar glanced from the long, curved blade of that weapon to the slender needle gripped in Clarinda's white-knuckled hand.

His olive-skinned face split in a grin, revealing several dazzling white teeth and one gleaming gold one placed squarely in the center of his mouth. He threw back his head with a bellow of laughter. The other men were quick to join in, making it clear the joke was at Clarinda's expense.

When the man spoke, his voice was a hearty boom, but his English was as sound as her own. "'Twould be a shame to skewer a creature with such spirit. She'll fetch a pretty price at market." He looked her up and down, the assessing gleam in his eyes making her feel as if she were already standing naked and shivering on some slaver's block. "There are many men in this world who would pay a king's ransom just for the pleasure of breaking her."

At that moment a gust of wind snatched the hat from Clarinda's head. Her hair came tumbling out of its combs and around her shoulders in a spill of wheaten silk.

The Corsairs breathed an appreciative chorus of oohs and aahs. A man with the face of a malnourished weasel and two broken and blackened front teeth actually stretched out a hand as if to touch her hair, his eyes glazed and his jaw slack with longing. Before his dirt-encrusted fingertips could brush a single strand, Clarinda jabbed the hatpin deep into the tender pad between his thumb and forefinger.

Letting out a howl, the pirate drew back his wounded hand as if to backhand her. The giant gave him a casual cuff, laying him out flat on the deck with no more effort than it would have taken for an ordinary man to swat a gnat.

"Keep your filthy paws to yourself," the giant growled. "I do not want any marks on the merchandise."

The tender smile he turned on Clarinda was even more terrifying than his snarl. Deprived of her meager weapon, she began to back away from him once again with Poppy still clinging to her back like a barnacle.

The hitch of a sob in her friend's breath echoed her own growing despair. "Oh, if only Captain Sir Ashton Burke was here!" Poppy moaned. "I just know such a man could save us!"

As the half circle of pirates advanced on them, their swarthy faces still glistening with the sweat of battle and their dark eyes gleaming with a chilling combination of lust and bloodlust, an even more violent gust of wind tore Captain Burke's likeness from Clarinda's numb fingers. The sketch went sailing over the ship's rail, borne away on the wings of the wind.

"That's the problem with heroes, Poppy," she said grimly. "There's never one around when you need one."

Continue reading for an exclusive
sneak preview of the next thrilling historical
romance from Teresa Medeiros

The Temptation of Your Touch

Coming in early 2013 from Pocket Books

*M*aximillian Burke was a very bad man.

He watched a tendril of smoke rise from the mouth of the pistol in his hand, trying to figure out exactly when he had embraced the role of villain in the farce his life had become. He had always been the honorable one, the dependable one, the one who chose each step he took with the utmost care to avoid even the possibility of a stumble. He had spent his entire life striving to be the son every father would be proud to claim and the man any mother would want her daughter to marry.

At least that's what everyone believed.

It was his younger brother who had gone around getting into brawls, challenging drunken loudmouths to duels, and facing the occasional firing squad. But now his brother was comfortably settled in their ancestral home of Dryden Hall with his adoring wife and their chattering moppet of a daughter. A daughter who had her mother's flaxen hair and laughing green eyes.

Maximillian briefly closed his eyes, as if by doing so he could blot out the image.

While his brother enjoyed the domestic bliss that should have been Max's with the woman Max had loved for most of his life, Max stood in a chilly Hyde Park meadow at dawn, his boots coated with wet grass and the man he had just shot groaning on the ground twenty paces away.

He had little doubt his brother would have laughed at his predicament, even if it had been a drunken slur cast on Max's sister-in-law's good name that had prompted it.

Max could not seem to remember that her honor was no longer his to defend.

When he opened his gray eyes, they were as steely as flints. "Get up and stop whining, you fool!" he told the man still writhing about on the grass. "The wound isn't mortal. I only winged your shoulder."

Clutching his upper arm in bloodstained fingers, the young swell eyed Max reproachfully, his ragged sniff making Max fear he was about to burst into tears. "You needn't be so unkind, my lord. It still hurts like the devil."

Blowing out an impatient sigh, Max handed the pistol to the East India Company lieutenant he had bullied into being his second and stalked across the grass to help the wounded man to his feet, gentling his grip with tremendous effort. "It's going to hurt more if you lie there whimpering until a constable comes to toss us both into Newgate for the crime of dueling. It will probably fester in that filth and you'll lose the arm altogether."

Max was only too relieved to hand the wounded fellow off to the man's white-faced second and the hovering surgeon. Resting his hands on his hips, Max watched them load the lad into a carriage.

He had to confess, there was something almost liberating about relinquishing his heroic mantle. When you were a villain, no one looked at you askance if you drank too much or neglected to tie your cravat in a flawless bow. No one whispered behind a hand if it had been three days since your last shave. Max ruefully stroked the stubble on his jaw, remembering a time when he would have fired his valet for letting him appear in public in such a disreputable state.

Since resigning from the board of the East India Company, he was no longer forced to make painfully polite conversation with those who sought his favor. Nor did he have to suffer fools graciously, if not gladly. Instead, everyone scurried out of his way to avoid the caustic lash of his tongue and the contempt smoldering in his smoky gray eyes. They had no way of knowing his contempt wasn't for them, but for the man he had become, the man he had always secretly been.

If Max hadn't been so deep in his cups when he had overheard his unfortunate dueling opponent loudly tell his friends that Max's brother had married a sultan's whore, he would have never challenged the silly git to a duel. What the boy really needed was a sound thrashing before being sent to bed without supper.

Shaking his head in disgust, Max turned on his heel and went striding toward his own carriage. He needed to get out of London before he killed someone. Most likely himself.

The lieutenant hurried back across the grass to retrieve the pistol and return it to its mahogany case before trotting after him. "M-m-my lord?" he asked, a stammer betraying his nervousness. "W-where are you going?"

"Probably hell," Max snapped without breaking his stride. "All that remains to be seen is how long it will take me to get there."